small as an elephant

small as an elephant

JENNIFER RICHARD JACOBSON

CANDLEWICK PRESS

Copyright © 2011 by Jennifer Richard Jacobson

First edition 2011

Excerpt from *The Magician's Elephant* (page 254) copyright © 2009 by Kate DiCamillo. Reproduced by permission of the publisher, Candlewick Press, Somerville, MA.

Library of Congress Cataloging-in-Publication Data

Jacobson, Jennifer, date.
Small as an elephant / Jennifer Richard Jacobson. — 1st U.S. ed.
p. cm.
Summary: Abandoned by his mother in an Acadia National Park campground, Jack tries to make his way back to Boston before anyone figures out what is going on, with only a small toy elephant for company.
ISBN 978-0-7636-4155-9
[1. Abandoned children — Fiction. 2. Mothers and sons — Fiction.
3. Self-reliance — Fiction. 4. Adventure and adventurers — Fiction.
5. Survival — Fiction. 6. New England — Fiction.] I. Title.
PZ7.J1529Sm 2011
[Fic] — dc22   2010039175

13 14 15 BVG 10 9 8 7

Printed in Berryville, VA, U.S.A.

This book was typeset in Bembo.

Candlewick Press
99 Dover Street
Somerville, Massachusetts 02144

visit us at www.candlewick.com

For Holly and Erik

One

If anyone wants to know what elephants are
like, they are like people, only more so.
— PETER CORNEILLE

Elephants can sense danger. They're able to detect
an approaching tsunami or earthquake before it hits.
Unfortunately, Jack did not have this talent. The
day his life was turned completely upside down, he
was caught unaware.

He was in a little Hubba tent at Seawall Campground, on Mount Desert Island. The night had
been cool, and Jack had been glad he'd insisted
on taking his warmer sleeping bag when his mom
tried to talk him into the other one, the one that
was lighter and easier to scrunch up.

But now it was morning, and he was hot. His sweat-soaked hair stuck to his neck and forehead. Clothes dryer — that's what the tent smelled like: a trapped-heat smell that filled his nostrils and told him the sun was high. *It's gotta be lunchtime,* he thought, kicking off his sleeping bag. Why hadn't she woken him up? He raced the tent zipper around its track and scrambled out into fresher air.

Dang!

The rental car was gone! He stood there, rooted, as if his eyes just had to adjust to the light, had to let forms take shape, and the car would be there, right where she'd left it. But the car was really gone. So was the little tent his mother had pitched on the gravelly ground next to his.

Jack tried to take a deep breath, but the air outside was now as heavy and suffocating as the air inside the tent had been.

Had she moved sites? Maybe the ground beneath her sleeping bag was too rocky and she'd decided to find a better site. Which would make sense, he suddenly realized, because the camping gear they'd spread across the picnic table was no longer there, either.

All that was left on the site was Jack and his Hubba.

He fumbled for his phone to call her. No reception in the campground—at least not in this spot.

Relax, he told himself. It probably had nothing to do with what had happened yesterday. A softer site—or one closer to the ocean—had probably opened up. She'd jumped on it and was now sitting there, looking out at the Atlantic, waiting for him to show up.

From what they'd been told, cars lined up every morning to get a spot at this campground—first come, first served. But Jack and his mother hadn't come at dawn. In fact, they hadn't arrived until late last night, and the ranger who explained the system said they were lucky—a family had just left because of a sick kid. Jack figured his mom got back in line first thing this morning to see what else was available. This was their summer vacation, and they were planning on camping here in Acadia National Park for three nights. She'd want it to be extra special.

Question was, should he pack up his tent and

take it with him? Or find her first? His stomach growled; he'd look now and pack later.

Like most campgrounds, this one had lots of looping roads twisting through the woods. Jack began with Loop A and Loop B, figuring those would have sites on the water. But unless he was mistaken, or had missed a road or two, *none* of the campsites had ocean views. So he scoped Loop C and Loop D, slowly enough to get a good look at the sites, fast enough to not look suspicious. Lots of places had a single tent, and since Jack's mother had borrowed both of the tents they were using, and because they had pitched them in the dark, Jack couldn't even say for sure what his mom's tent looked like. So he stuck to looking for the rental car.

His mother had specifically asked for a Prius. Not just because they were traveling all the way from Boston to Maine and gas was expensive, but because she believed in doing what she could to save the earth.

"So what does this car run on?" Jack had asked. "Biodiesel?"

"Nope. Gas and electricity."

"You can make energy from elephant poop,

you know," Jack had said. "The Dallas Zoo calls it poo power!"

"P-U, talk about *biogas*!" his mother had said.

He'd laughed. His mother was so quick with one-liners.

Him? He was an expert on all things elephant.

Right now he wished he had the memory of an elephant. Was the car white or silver? Walking in circles suddenly felt ridiculous, so when he passed his own tent for the second time (it being on the only campsite with one tent and *nothing* else), he decided to stop looking. Instead, he reached into his pocket, pulled out his spending money, and tossed it onto the picnic table. Fourteen dollars and sixty-three cents. He was going to find food.

There were no concession stands in the campground, no restaurants — not even a convenience store — so Jack jogged out to the registration hut and asked the woman behind the counter (who was reading a fantasy by Robin McKinley, the same one his friend Nina had read earlier this summer) where the nearest market was.

"Tired of Dinty Moore?" she asked. "Seawall Camping Supplies. Right down the road."

Jack knew all about Dinty Moore stew—not from camping, but from the nights when his mom had to work late and he made his own dinner. "Do you know if—" He was going to say, *If a woman with short blond hair and a light-colored Prius has come through,* but a feeling in the pit of his stomach made him change his mind midsentence. "If that store you just mentioned has those bright—those neon-red hot dogs?"

The woman laughed. "Red snappers! Absolutely!"

Jack smiled. As least one of the things his mom had promised on the drive to Maine was going to happen. He was going to bite into a glowing red hot dog and hear a *snap.*

The first thing Jack did once he'd left the park and was on Route 102A was pull out his phone again. There was a single bar—he had a tiny chance of reaching his mother. He punched in the number. Yes! It was ringing!

But she didn't pick up. He wished they hadn't argued in the car last night. He wished he'd tried to be a little more understanding.

He hung up and tried again, this time listening to her voice-mail message: "Becky Martel here—or *not* here, to be exact. Don't leave any old message. Wow me!"

He waited for the beep and then shouted, "Where are you?"

Two

Separated elephants keep in touch with infrasonic calls, sounds too low-pitched for humans to hear.

Seawall Camping Supplies didn't look like any store Jack had ever visited. It was a cabin—with a porch and everything—and had signs all over it. HOT SHOWERS AND LOBSTER POUND, read one sign. Another said, IT'S COOLER ON THE COAST. He would have felt nervous about walking into the strange place if not for a third sign that read, COIN-OP SHOWERS INSIDE STORE. CHANGE AT THE COUNTER. The sign made him laugh, and he wished his mother was there to share the joke.

A rack of stuffed animals greeted him just inside the door: lobsters, seals, moose, and black bears—but no elephants. The decklike wooden floor creaked as he ambled—among maps and maple syrup, fishing line and Goldfish crackers, all jumbled together—to the counter, where a woman in an apron was waiting to take his order.

"How much are the hot dogs?" Jack asked.

"You can have two dogs, chips, and a small soda for four dollars," she said.

"Red ones?"

"Of course. What do you want on 'em?"

"Mustard," he said, taking a five out of his pocket and then, before handing it over, asking, "Can I buy a paper, too?"

The woman nodded at the pile of newspapers by the door and added the price of a *Bangor Daily News*.

Jack sat down at a table on the porch to wait and scanned the headlines, barely giving himself enough time to read the words. *Breathe,* he reminded himself after a moment, the way his mother would. *What's the worst that could have happened?*

Car accident. Definitely. The only thing he knew for sure was that his mother had taken the car. She'd taken the Prius and had headed off somewhere this morning (*Last night? As soon as I fell asleep?*) and, although she was a good driver—in fact, that was her job, driving a shuttle for the Intown Inn—he figured anyone could speed off these twisty island roads.

BLACK BEARS caught his eye, but it was an article about a football team and not wild animals. Another headline, about a missing nine-year-old girl, stopped him. (Did adults get kidnapped?) Jack was reading this story when the woman brought his food.

"Scary, isn't it?" she said, glancing down at the paper. "Sure hope they find her safe and sound."

Jack nodded, thinking about his mom and pushing the paper away. He took a bite of his hot dog and heard the snap—the snap his mom had told him about, the snap *she* was supposed to show him . . . show him and laugh about. *She* was supposed to show him the hot dog's thick casing and its candy-apple color, then they were supposed to laugh and eat and talk about the first time she'd ever had a red hot dog in Maine.

He felt heaviness in his arms and put the hot dog down. Dang it! These were supposed to be the best three days of his whole summer. The ones that were going to make up for all the boring days he'd spent in their nothing-to-do apartment. Mom, in her exploding firecracker way, had borrowed equipment, read online reviews, made lists of all the best places to visit, circled maps, and even downloaded music for the car ride. She could hardly stop talking about Sand Beach, Thunder Hole, and all the other great things she wanted him to see on this trip.

Where was she? Why had she taken off when they already had more things on their list than they could possibly do? He could imagine her going off to get something—some last-minute thing they needed to make this trip *absolutely perfect*—and then meeting someone interesting. Someone who made art out of sea sponges, or wrote the messages in juice-bottle caps. She would be unable to pull herself away. "Can you believe it, Jack?" she'd say. "He sits in an office all day, thinking up what to write inside the tops of bottles."

Yeah, OK. But why take the tent?

She would have some train of reasoning, no doubt: first she thought *this,* and then *that* occurred to her, but then . . . It would be one thought sparking another, until all the ideas burst into flames—or so it seemed to Jack. It didn't even make sense to try and figure it out; he knew that by now. Sometimes he couldn't even follow the thoughts *after* she explained.

And now a whole morning was shot. Well, he wasn't going to just sit around and wait, not this time, dang it. She could go off and have her amazing time—he was going to have his own adventure. He was on Mount Desert Island, and he hadn't even put his toes in the ocean yet. He'd change that.

He cleared off his table—leaving the newspaper for someone else to read—and walked across the street to where lots of people had pulled over to escape their cars and teeter along the tumbling, rocky shore.

The day was growing steamy, and the ocean air smelled like warm olives. Jack bounced from the dry, sea-worn stones down to the darker, seaweed-covered boulders below. As he did, he couldn't help examining each group of tourists—the large family with the grandfather holding on to the shoulders of twin boys to balance himself; two girls in green camp T-shirts who stood outside their camp group, uninterested in the wildlife in a tidal pool; a bunch of older women sitting around a flat rock as if it were a table and sipping something from a thermos — all the while searching for his tall, willowy mother, her cropped blond hair. He didn't bother to search the more remote edges of the beach; she hated being alone.

A boy about Jack's age, eleven, but with shorter hair and a wide smile of bright white teeth, was tossing a Frisbee with his little sister. The girl's long blond hair whipped across her face as she flung the disk into the air. Neither had much of a throw; the Frisbee kept smacking nearby rocks, sometimes getting wedged between them. It didn't matter. It was impossible to run on this treacherous beach, and both of them laughed at the senselessness of the game. So did their parents, who were watching from stone chairs.

Jack wished he could be that boy, a kid who had nothing more to worry about than where his Frisbee landed. A boy who could make his parents happy just by playing a silly game.

Then he immediately took it back. His mom was cool. Real cool. Cooler than a lot of other moms. He promised himself he'd tell her that when she returned.

She definitely wasn't on this beach. Should he go back to the campsite in case she was there? *Nah,* he thought. *She'd know to look for me here.* He'd stay, give her time to come down. He imagined her sneaking up behind him, surprising him here.

He took off his sneakers and socks, then peeled off his shirt and carefully wrapped his phone inside it. He tucked the bundle in a dry crevice of a fairly large boulder. Maybe once he got down to where the tide had receded, he'd even be brave enough to swim. (Though it didn't look as if anyone else was even thinking about going near the foamy, churning water.)

At the first bright algae-green tidal pool he came to, Jack picked up a snail and examined its shell. Then he crouched, preparing to pick up a crab.

"It'll pinch you."

Jack looked up. The Frisbee kid and his sister had come up beside him.

"Not if I pick it up from behind," said Jack. He

carefully positioned his fingers on the back of the crab's shell.

The boy's sister squealed as Jack lifted the crab into the air. It waved its pincers frantically.

"He's so big!" said the girl. "Isn't he, Aiden?"

Used to be huge until the Elephant Child shrank it, thought Jack, remembering a story his mother had told him.

Eventually, Jack let the crab go, and without saying a word, he and Aiden leaped from one slippery rock to the next toward the water, while Aiden's sister wandered back toward her parents. They dipped their feet into the freezing-cold sea until Aiden's parents called them away from the dangerous surf, and then they whipped seaweed at each other's legs instead.

Jack imagined his mother standing on the shore, watching, smiling at their foolishness.

He started to ask Aiden if he wanted to build a castle out of the rocks, when Aiden's father called down to say they were leaving.

"Are you staying at the campground?" he asked instead.

Aiden nodded.

"Me too," Jack said.

"Maybe we'll see you at the ranger's talk tonight," Aiden replied, then ran to catch up with his parents.

Jack watched Aiden's family gather their things and walk away together. Aiden's mom draped her arm over Aiden's shoulder. Jack walked over to his shirt and checked his phone, praying for a message.

Nothing.

He scanned the beach one more time, hoping to see her face.

No such luck.

It's OK, he told himself, tucking his phone back into his pocket. *It hasn't been* that *long.* He looked down at the rocks on the beach, the rocks that only an hour or so ago had been almost completely underwater. As he looked at them now, he saw something: a bird's-eye view of elephants, a whole herd of them. The smooth, darker rocks were grayish brown, some with speckles. One particularly rounded rock looked just like the back of the leader. That rock called to him.

Jack climbed back down and lay upon its warm surface.

He remembered the first time his mother had taken him to see an elephant. He had been really little, no older than four. They'd been at a circus, and he'd hated it—hated the chaotic music, the sudden snap of the ringmaster's whip, the diamond-eyed clowns. So she'd carried him away from all that and into another tent, a tent where the most enormous animal he'd ever seen stood only a few feet away. Jack had whimpered and buried his face in his mother's neck, but he couldn't resist peeking at the huge creature. And then the elephant had reached toward him with her trunk, reached toward him and tapped him on the shoulder. He'd squealed and plunged back under the cover of his mother's chin. But the elephant had tapped him again, and kept on tapping him till he lifted his head and looked over at her. Slowly, slowly, she'd reached out her trunk again and touched his cheek. Jack remembered giggling, remembered feeling as if the elephant tent were the safest place in the world.

Jack lay facedown on that rock until he'd pulled every last bit of heat from it, and then he meandered back to the campground. He strolled past the wooden registration hut, with its pointy roof and welcoming porch (no Prius in the parking lot), past the signs below towering trees that directed drivers to the proper loop in the thick, scrubby woods, past the entrance to the outdoor amphitheater, to A-loop. He decided to take the long way around the circle. He told himself that if he was extra patient, if he remained calm and hopeful, if he walked slowly enough around the shady A-loop, checking each and every site for the car, his mom would be back.

As he turned to the right, he heard Aiden's voice and his little sister's, too—Julie, he remembered Aiden calling her—and realized that they were the family that had hung an enormous blue tarp over their entire campsite, protecting it from rain. He was tempted to pop through the brush that made their site particularly private and say hi, but didn't want to draw too much attention to himself, didn't want Aiden's parents to start wondering who this kid was, anyway, and why he was just hanging out, all alone.

Plus, he didn't want to break the spell.

But it wasn't to be. His Hubba was still the only thing on his site.

"Anything wrong?"

Jack jumped. He'd been so intent on seeing his mom—willing her to appear right there at the picnic table, waiting for his return—that he hadn't heard the park ranger come up behind him.

She was dressed in a gray uniform with a badge and carried a clipboard. Her face was slightly wrinkled; her eyes were kind.

At this point, any other kid would tell the ranger that his mother was missing, that he had no idea what had happened to her. Then the adults would take over. They'd ask questions and put out a missing-person report. Someone would take him in and feed him dinner while they looked for her. And they'd probably find her. If not tonight, then soon.

But Jack wasn't any kid. And his mom wasn't just any mom.

"Nope," said Jack, placing his hands in his pockets. "Everything's good."

Three

*In Germany, captive elephants eat holiday leftovers:
Christmas trees! Each elephant consumes
about five Christmas trees a day.*

It wasn't much past six, and the sun was already setting. Jack needed a plan. He figured he could eat at the camping supply store again, but maybe it would be smarter if he bought a few groceries and brought them back instead.

And a fire would be sweet. A fire would add light (although he did have his flashlight, he reminded himself) and warmth. And he could cook something on it . . . or he could if he had some pots and pans. Which he didn't.

Marshmallows. A stick was all you needed to cook those. He'd buy one or two healthy things, something to drink, and marshmallows for toasting. Wouldn't his mom be surprised when she rolled in and saw him sitting there in front of the fire, popping a perfectly browned marshmallow into his mouth! He might just turn to her and say, "Want one?"

"Smell you!" she'd say, which was her way of saying, *You are one cool kid, Jack Martel.*

Jack liked imagining these scenes, even though he knew, in truth, he'd leap up and demand that she tell him where she'd been. And then she'd say something like, "I knew you'd be fine, Jackie," to make him feel better, but it wouldn't. Just the opposite. And then he'd be so mad, and at the same time so relieved, that he'd start to cry. So instead of being all OK and independent, he'd look like some helpless little kid.

This time he jogged out of the campground. He was nervous about bumping into the same ranger — not sure if he could keep his voice steady, keep his eyes conveying cheerfulness. As soon as he got onto the beat-up island road, he tried calling his mother again. Still no answer.

This time it was a guy with a mustache and a baseball cap behind the counter at Seawall Camping Supplies. *Be natural,* Jack told himself. *Kids probably come in here by themselves all the time. No big deal, right?* He gave the guy a quick nod (which felt more nerdy than cool) and checked out his options. He decided on salami, cheese, marshmallows, and orange juice, but when he added them up, they came to more than ten dollars. He had a little over nine. What to give up?

He was still trying to decide when he looked over at the coffee station and saw paper cups. Maybe they'd be willing to give him a cup, or sell it to him for ten cents or something, and he could get water out of the tap at the campground. Then he wouldn't need to buy the orange juice.

"Hey, OK if I take a cup?"

"No problem," the guy said. "Take one. Heck, take two."

So he put the orange juice back, then walked to the counter with the rest of his supplies. As the guy was ringing him up, Jack saw a display of matchbooks on the counter. He'd need something to light a fire with if he planned on roasting marshmallows. "Do those cost anything?" he asked, pointing to the matchbooks.

"Twelve dollars," said the guy.

Jack's mouth fell open.

"Nah, just kidding. Free—free to people who buy butts—but you can have one."

Jack used all but a few coins to pay for his groceries and then started out the door.

"Hey!" shouted the guy.

Jack's heart pounded. Did he do something wrong? Take something by accident?

"You won't burn anything down with those, right?"

Jack stopped and held up the marshmallows from his bag.

"Oh, yeah," said the guy. "Cool."

As he walked back past the registration hut, thinking about toasting his Jet Puffs, Jack suddenly remembered the sign he'd read inside when he and his mother had registered last night: COLLECTING FIREWOOD IN PARK PROHIBITED. It was hard to believe they meant it; the woods along the campground road were full of dead wood, low branches on trees that had died, sticks covering the ground. It was all right there for the taking. Wouldn't it be helping them to gather some of this brush? The woods would look neater. . . . Did he dare?

Maybe he'd just hunt around his own campsite, where he wouldn't be so obvious.

He glanced toward the site where Aiden's family was staying. He could hear Julie talking in a hyper, squeaky way and the others laughing. Jack thought about walking over and just saying, "Hey, you're going to the talk tonight, right? The schedule at the gate says it's about owls. . . ." but he knew Aiden's parents would start asking the usual questions, which he'd have to answer carefully:

Where're you from?

Boston—Jamaica Plain. (He liked answering *Jamaica Plain* before people had the chance to say *What part?* which was what they always asked, even if they'd visited Boston only one time.)

Are you camping with your family?

My mom.

Where's your dad? (Julie would probably be the one to ask this.)

He'd settle on the truth. He'd had enough practice lying to know it was best to tell the truth whenever possible. *I don't have one.*

Would you and your mom like to join us? (That would probably be Aiden's mom.)

She's not feeling well, he'd say. That was as close to the truth as he could come.

But the imaginary conversation made him tired—tired of thinking, tired of trying to figure things out. Definitely too tired to risk talking to Aiden's family.

On the way back to his campsite, he passed bundles of wood for sale—only two dollars—but he was out of money. His mother had better pay him back tomorrow; that was his souvenir money he'd spent on food. Buying food was *her* responsibility.

He slipped into his tent, ripped open the food packaging with his teeth, and ate salami-and-cheese sandwiches without the bread. *Hors d'oeuvres,* he thought. Then he stuffed a handful of raw marshmallows into his mouth and closed his eyes.

"Baby elephant," he heard his grandmother saying. He was five, and they were sitting at a table. He had just stuffed his sandwich crusts into his mouth.

"Baby elephant," she'd said.

"Elephants *have* to stuff their faces," he'd said with a full mouth.

"I know," she said. "You told me. Three hundred pounds of food a day."

It was his earliest memory of his grandmother. Was it truly a memory or a story he'd heard his mom tell? He wasn't sure.

Once, Jack had asked his mother if they were ever going to see his grandmother again.

"Never!" Mom had said, wiping her face. She'd been crying a lot that day. "I'll never forgive that woman for what she tried to do to me—to *us,* Jackie."

They were sitting together in the multicolored hammock Mom had hung from the ceiling of the dining room—a room they had never used before the hammock. She had her favorite poetry book in her lap; he had woven his toes in and out of the soft hammock strings and was reading *The Cowboy and*

His Elephant. It was a book for adults, but he could read it—and liked it.

"Of course you can read a book for grown-ups, Jack. You're a smart kid," his mom had said. "Read a chapter to me."

He had, skipping over a bad word or two, and she had smiled.

Four

Elephants swim underwater by snorkeling: holding
their trunks just above the surface to breathe.

Jack woke feeling as if someone had glued his
tongue to the roof of his mouth. According to his
phone, it was nine p.m., only a couple of hours later.
He hadn't meant to fall asleep. He'd been lying
there, playing stupid games: If he could remember all the names of the sixteen Hawthorn-owned
elephants, his mother would come back. Or if he
could remember the names of the rescued elephants
at the Tennessee sanctuary, his mother would come
back. Or if he could remember which elephants at
the Tennessee sanctuary were Hawthorn elephants,

his mother would come back. But he'd dozed off, and now the salami and cheese had left him dying of thirst. He grabbed the two cups he'd gotten from the convenience store and headed down the road to find the tap. A full moon, rather than his flashlight, lit the way.

Aiden's mother was at the faucet; he recognized her red hair, pulled back in a ponytail. For a moment he thought of turning back, waiting until she left, but he was afraid he'd already been seen and didn't want to appear more conspicuous. He stood nearby, and he waited until she had filled her pot with rushing water before saying hi.

"You're the boy from the beach today," she said. "Jack, isn't it?"

He nodded.

"Aiden was thrilled to find you. I wouldn't let him bring a friend. Told him he'd meet kids on the road, but he didn't believe me."

Jack smiled and filled one of his cups. He gulped down the water, knowing his grandmother would accuse him of being rude, but he had to have water immediately. Maybe it wasn't just the salami; maybe it was the hot dogs and the sun and the salty sea, too, but Jack had never in his whole life felt so thirsty.

"Who are you camping with?" she asked. There was the question.

"My mother," he said, wiping his mouth with the hand that held the second cup. "I'm getting water for her, too," he said, lifting the two cups (like a little kid would, he thought later) and bending to fill them both.

"We're going to Echo Lake tomorrow. Would you and your mother like to join us? I know Aiden would certainly be happier."

Jack was glad he had two cups to fill; it gave him more time to think. He and his mom would have a ton of things to do tomorrow, all the stuff that had been on their list—that is, assuming she came back tonight, or first thing tomorrow morning. Which she probably would.

But what if she *didn't*? Nothing would be worse than sitting around, waiting for her. Besides, it would serve her right to wonder where he was.

"My mother's not feeling well, but I'd like to come. I'll ask her if it's OK," he said.

"Great!" she said. "Would you like me to walk back with you?"

"No—thanks, though. I think I'm just going to stand here and empty the well," he said. "Or the reservoir, or whatever."

"OK, then," she said. "Good night."

An ache in his chest, an ache he didn't even know he had, started to lift. Maybe a good-night from a mother—from anyone's mother—was all he needed.

The next morning, Jack woke to the wheezy cooing of a mourning dove and felt happy—for about two seconds. Then he remembered. He listened, hoping to hear his mother moving around the site, whistling "Sunny Days" from *Sesame Street,* like she always did, but he knew better. She wouldn't have waited for Jack to wake on his own. She'd have circled the tent, pretending to be a coyote or something. Then she'd have pounced on him, taking the whole tent down with her. She'd crawl into the collapsed tent and hug him, finally telling him where she'd been. He would push her away, but it wouldn't work. "Don't be mad at me, Jack," she'd say. "I could never leave you."

"Like an elephant," he whispered now. Even when in danger, a mother elephant would not leave her calf.

He looked at his phone to check the time and noticed that not only did he still not have reception, but the battery was about to die. The charger was in the car—the car his mother had taken. He turned his phone off.

The tent smelled sour. No doubt he should take a shower, but he probably didn't have enough coins to use the showers in the camping-supplies store. And anyway, he was going swimming with Aiden's family. He grabbed what was left of the salami and cheese and sat out on the picnic table to have breakfast.

The early-morning air was cool. A mother in her pajamas, clutching a towel and a cosmetics kit, was leading two young girls to the bathroom.

"Do you want eggs?" he heard the man in the next site ask his family.

"Yes, please!" his mother would have called back, and before you knew it, she'd be over there helping with the cooking.

Jack noticed a ranger, a man this time, with a green jacket over his gray uniform, walking purposefully around the loop, and his breakfast caught in his throat. What should he do? Duck back into his tent? The bathroom?

Too late. The ranger skipped his neighbors and came directly into his site.

"Hey, there," said the ranger. "Is your mom here?"

Jack shook his head. "She's just gone to the store—to pick up stuff." He hoped the ranger hadn't noticed that the car (and his mother) had been gone since yesterday morning.

The ranger nodded. Jack couldn't tell if he believed him or not.

"Well," he said, "I just want to confirm that you're here until tomorrow."

"Yup," said Jack. Wherever his mom had gone, she'd have to come back by tomorrow. Right?

"Can we stay longer if we want?" he blurted, hoping he sounded enthusiastic and not worried.

"Sure. The park really clears out after Labor Day. They'll be no shortage of spaces then. Just remember, you need to prepay."

"I'll tell my mother," he said, hoping it was the end of the conversation.

"OK, then," said the ranger, in no hurry to go. "My name's Stan, if you need anything."

Jack wondered if Stan was thinking the obvious: Tuesday, the day after Labor Day, was the first day of school. At least it was for Jack. Why would they want to camp longer?

But the ranger glanced at his clipboard and went on. Jack ate the last bite of salami and then wished he hadn't. This was the only food he had, and he'd spent all his money. He had to start being smarter. Start thinking about the possibility —

He stopped that thought in its tracks. *Don't be ridiculous,* he told himself. *Mom will be back today. I know she will.* Just the same, he wrapped the remaining cheese.

A stick cracked behind him. Jack turned hopefully.

Not Mom. Aiden — and a cold splash of disappointment.

"Ready to go?"

Jack popped back into his tent, changed into his

suit, and slipped his phone into his pocket. But as he and Aiden began to leave the site, Aiden seemed to hesitate.

Jack suddenly saw the site — one little tent, no car — from Aiden's eyes. "My mom's gone to get coffee," Jack said. "Even when she's sick, she needs coffee."

Aiden laughed. "Sounds like my dad," he said, and turned to lead Jack back to his site.

Jack had expected to ride in the family car to Echo Lake. Instead, they took the Island Explorer, a free bus that went all around Mount Desert Island.

"It's better for the environment. Better for the island," explained Aiden's dad. "Cuts down on traffic and exhaust, uses less gas."

It wasn't the environment Jack was thinking about as he bounced a little in his seat, studying the map of the Island Explorer route. He realized that he now had a way — a *free* way — to search for his mom.

During a lull in the conversation, Jack took out his phone and tried again to reach his mom. This time, he got her voice mail immediately. That meant she had turned off her phone. Which meant that she probably hadn't driven off the road and gotten stuck in a ditch somewhere.

Which meant that she could have called him. . . .

No, it didn't mean just that one thing. Her battery could have died. If something had happened to her, if she was lying unconscious somewhere, her phone could very well be dead.

Jack gazed out the window and caught himself looking for tire marks or any other signs that a car had skidded off the road.

What if she was in trouble? What if she was like that woman who somehow drove into a ravine and survived for a whole week in her car without food? Mom had told him the story. Said the woman had raised her arm out the window and caught rainwater from overhanging leaves. Maybe he should tell someone, like Aiden's mom or dad. Tell them his mother was missing and was maybe hurt, needing help. Maybe he should tell them right now —

But he didn't.

He didn't tell them because a car accident was

not the likeliest of all the possibilities. The likeliest possibility was that she had just gone off—again.

The last time had been at home, and he had just stayed in the apartment, and there was food, and there were things to do, and he hadn't told anyone, and she had come home, and no one had to get involved, and no one asked too many questions, and no one had tried to take him away.

So Jack didn't tell Aiden's parents. But he made a promise to himself: he would look for her, and if he didn't find her on the island, *then* he would tell someone. Or at least he would think seriously about telling someone.

He was relieved when the bus pulled into the little parking lot at Echo Lake. There wasn't anything he could do now—not if he wasn't going to tell anyone—so he decided he might as well enjoy the few hours they had here.

They walked down a boardwalk to a small, sandy beach. Aiden's family gravitated to the far left, at the trees' edge, where rocks formed a cozy nook and there was shade. Aiden's dad set up two small beach chairs he'd been carrying. Aiden's mom spread out a blanket on the sand and unzipped a soft cooler of food. "Would you like something to eat, Jack?" she asked.

Jack suddenly realized he'd been staring at the cooler and felt his face go warm. His stomach was cavernous, demanding more than a few slices of cheese and salami.

"Let's swim first," said Aiden, turning and running into the water.

Jack followed reluctantly.

When they tired of swim races, jumping off rocks (ignoring the KEEP OFF THE ROCKS sign like everyone else), and trying to do backflips in the water, they staggered back to the blanket. Aiden's mom had spread out tuna fish sandwiches, grapes, apples, carrots, chips, pickles, and double-chocolate brownies. Jack couldn't remember a time when food had tasted so good. She slipped another sandwich onto his plate without even asking.

By the time he got to the brownies, he was feeling full, but no way was he going to refuse these. He took a bite and lay back in the sand, letting the chocolate melt in his mouth.

"There's a herd of elephants," Jack said, point-ing straight up.

"Huh?" asked Aiden.

"In the sky," Jack told him. "A herd of elephants."

"I see one there!" said Julie. "Look, there's its trunk!"

Everyone tried to see where Julie was pointing.

"I see it!" shouted Aiden's mom.

"There's an elephant stretched out on its belly!" said Aiden.

"That's so weird," said Aiden's dad. "If you think about elephants, you see them everywhere."

Jack smiled. He and his mother could point out elephants for hours. Sometimes they even found them alphabetically: Airy Elephant, Balloon Elephant, Curly Elephant . . . He missed his mom so much at that moment, that moment of cloud watching, that he could almost *feel* his thoughts traveling to her, and finding her, and making her pick up her phone.

"Excuse me," he said suddenly, jumping up and walking back up the boardwalk, in the direction of the restrooms. He didn't stop. He walked right past them and ducked into the woods. He pulled his phone out of his pocket, his heart pulsing with hope, and —

"No!" he shouted. *No! No! No!* How could he have been so stupid? He had forgotten. Forgotten that his phone was in his pocket. Forgotten and gone swimming! The phone was totally soaked. He pushed a few buttons, but it didn't even make its familiar beeping sounds. He held the On button for what seemed like three minutes with no luck at all. Totally soaked and totally dead.

The battery! He remembered that cell phones have a patch that tells whether they've been damaged by liquid. Whether the phone can be saved. He turned his phone over and slid his battery out. The patch was red. Ruined.

"No!" Jack threw the phone — screamed and threw it as far as he possibly could.

It was one thing to be able to leave his mom messages and wonder if she got them. But now she'd have no way of reaching him. What if he got kicked off the campsite tomorrow? How would his mom know where to find him? How would they possibly connect?

Jack lay down at the base of a tree and bawled.

Five

*Due to the thick padding on their
feet, elephants walk silently.*

Jack could tell that Aiden's parents knew something
was wrong when he returned to the picnic. He
tried to stay as close to the truth as possible, saying
he was worried about his mom—her not feeling
well and all.

"What was I thinking?" said Aiden's mom,
whose name, Jack had learned during lunch, was
Diane. "I should have checked in on her, asked her
if she needed anything."

"Oh, that's OK," Jack said quickly. "It was just

a migraine . . . I think." He had added that last bit, the "I think," because he didn't exactly know what a migraine was. But he'd seen commercials on TV, and it seemed like a sort of headache, but a really bad one.

"Well, I'll definitely check on her when we bring you back," Diane said.

Great, Jack. Now what?

It was impossible to have fun for the rest of the afternoon. He hated being away from the campsite now that he didn't have a phone. What if his mother returned and he wasn't there? What if she tried to call? He doubted she'd be able to reason, to stay put, to wait patiently as he had.

And then there was Diane's determination to check up on his mother. There was no way she'd keep his mom's disappearance a secret, no matter how hard he tried to convince her. She'd be just like the social workers and the guidance counselor and everyone else who thought they were helping when they were just making things worse.

He thought the veins in his head were going to burst as Aiden and his mother walked him back to his campsite.

"Huh. The car's gone," Jack announced as soon as they were in sight of his tent, hoping he sounded genuinely surprised. "She must have gone to get more medicine. She said she would probably have to do that."

"That's your tent?" Diane asked.

Jack could hear the other questions in her voice. None of the other sites looked like his—just a little Hubba tent and nothing else.

"She got sick as soon as we arrived," said Jack. "We never even bothered to unpack anything."

"You poor thing. Tell her that I'm making dinner tonight. I'll bring over soup—and other good things."

"Oh, that's OK." Jack suddenly felt as if he was on a speeding train, heading for a collision. "She'll probably bring us back some takeout."

"Doesn't matter," Diane said. "Soup goes with everything. Tell her I'll be back to see what she needs."

"OK." Even though he was getting used to lying, he couldn't figure out what to do next.

"Do you want to hang out till your mom gets back?" asked Aiden.

Diane smiled at Aiden. You could tell she thought he was doing the right thing.

"Thanks," said Jack, "but I'm good. I've got comics; I think I'll just read for a while."

After they left, Jack crawled into his tent to think. What would he say when they returned? Maybe he could pretend that his mom had *just* disappeared. That wasn't as big a deal as her having been gone since—when? Friday night? But what good would that do? There would be a big search. The story would be in the papers, just like that story about the missing girl. And he'd be taken from his mom for sure.

Once, when he was about seven, he and his mother were down in the subway station, waiting for the Forest Hills train to take them home. He was sitting on a bench, reading the advertisements on the wall across the tracks. His mom, who was wearing lots of silky scarves, was bouncing around, talking to people in the station. When he glanced over, he saw her whispering something into a homeless woman's ear. The woman smiled, rocked on her heels, and shouted gibberish.

"That's right!" his mother had said. "You're absolutely right! Jack!" she'd shouted. "Come here!"

Her voice had grown more—what? Jangly. Urgent. It was his mother's voice, but it wasn't his mother—at least, not the mother he loved best. He'd wanted to protect her, to pull her away from the strangers who had begun to watch her cautiously, and back to him. He'd gone over to her and, after a couple of attempts, caught one of her waving hands. "Mom," he'd said. "Come tell me what this word on a sign means."

She'd leaped out of his grasp. "Answer this riddle, Jack," she'd said, pulling a red scarf from around her waist and holding it up to the light. "What can burn in space?"

"The sun," he'd said quickly, wanting to get this over with.

"Oh, my smart, smart boy!" She'd rubbed the top of his head. "That's because the sun is made of oxygen. But can other things burn?"

He'd tried to think of an answer.

Then the homeless woman had reached out and grabbed his mother's scarf. Mom had snatched it back, laughed, and then bent down to wrap it around the woman's neck. "Burn, baby, burn!" his mom had said.

She'd danced around the station, demanding to know: "What can burn in space?"

Lots of people just turned away or put their hands up as if to say no to what she was selling. He'd followed her, trying to think; she might stop racing around if he could come up with the answer.

"What can burn in space?" she'd called out.

"A rocket?" a tall bald man had guessed, trying to play along.

For some reason that answer had made his mom frustrated. "Jack, help me. They won't listen," she'd said.

He'd tried really hard to figure out what it was that she was thinking, wanting to show her *he* understood. There was a song, she'd said, a song about a fire, they didn't start the fire, but they had to put it out . . . and she wanted to tell people, warn them. He'd kept asking questions so that she'd look straight at him.

But she'd jumped away from Jack and had

begun to pull on people's clothing to get them to pay attention.

"Lady!" a man had yelled.

"Mom, please," Jack had said, wrapping his arms around his mother's waist, trying to hold her in place.

The Forest Hills train had pulled in.

"Mom, look! Our train is here." The doors had slid open, and Jack had put his hands on her back and tried to drive her into the train, but she'd turned around fast, knocking him to the ground.

Soon after that, the police had come. They took his mom to the hospital, and he went first to DSS and then to his grandmother's.

Jack had heard of DSS. He knew they took kids away from bad mothers. What he didn't know until then was that his grandmother would try to take him, too.

She'd kept asking him questions, one after another. Mom had warned him about questions like this. Told him not to answer them from anyone— not his teacher or the social worker or his grandmother, especially his grandmother ("She can be evil, Jack," his mother had said)—and he had tried to keep quiet, tried not to say anything, but his grandmother wouldn't stop.

"You talk too much!" he'd finally shouted at her. And for a while she seemed to stop. But still she was there, watching him, staring at him, thinking about the questions she wanted to ask—he could tell. Eventually, he'd found places in her big house where he could hide from her until finally they let his mom go and she came to get him.

He couldn't let that happen again.

Springing to a crouched position, he rolled up his sleeping bag and stuffed it into his backpack. He added the flashlight, three comic books, and the cheese. He tried to add the few items of clothing he'd brought along, but there was no way it would all fit. He couldn't carry the tent or the borrowed air mattress he'd slept on, and now he'd have to leave clothes as well. Should he wear shorts or jeans? Shorts would be easier to walk in, he decided. But he grabbed one long-sleeved shirt and his Windbreaker and tied them around his waist. Then he rushed to collapse the tent around the remaining belongings and dragged the bundle into the woods, where, hopefully, it wouldn't be found for days.

He hesitated for a single moment, wishing more than anything that Mom would appear, would drive right up and say, "Hey, Jackie, where're you headed?" But it didn't happen.

So he threw on his backpack and hustled down the road to catch the Island Explorer again.

Six

He who mounts a wild elephant goes
where the wild elephant goes.
— RANDOLPH BOURNE

"Did you miss your stop?" the driver asked when Jack had reached the end of the bus line. He'd been riding the bus for almost an hour. The island was much bigger than he'd imagined, and he realized that searching for his mother would be harder—a lot harder—than he thought. Each time the bus stopped at a dock, or lake, or town, he wondered if this was the place where he should look first, but the bus always moved on before he made a decision.

"Son?"

What to do? Suddenly, he felt so tired. And now here he was in Bar Harbor—a town that had been on their list for all its fun shops and restaurants. A town that may or may not hold his mother.

I have to start my search somewhere, he figured, and got off the bus.

Standing in the village green, he realized that "searching" was not a plan. You couldn't just walk around a big island, hoping to find someone. He needed to do this logically. The sun was setting, and while he could try searching some of the shops and restaurants, he knew he had to be realistic, and being realistic meant finding a place to sleep while there was still some light left.

Obviously, he'd have to camp. Not at a campground, which cost money, but in the woods. He'd seen plenty of woods on the bus ride in. With one last look at the bustling streets, Jack turned and walked back out of town.

He walked for about ten minutes down Mount Desert Street, where he passed a stone church, a graveyard with lots of unmarked graves—or so the sign said—and the town library, to Kebo Street. On Kebo, he ducked into a patch of woods. Right away he found a mossy area in the roots of a tree, a soft place for sleeping that was far enough from the road that no one would notice him, but not so far in that he would get lost. He unrolled his dark-green sleeping bag and crawled in. Mom had said they might sleep under the stars one night, and now he was doing it. Check two things off the list!

He tried to come up with a plan. Maybe he should get a map of the town and comb all the streets. He could ask people who worked in the galleries and restaurants and shops if they'd seen her. Or ask at the grocery store—chances were, she'd stopped for something.

Thinking about Mom and the next steps made his brain hurt. So he let his heavy eyes shut, let snatches of dreams about winding roads, pine trees, anchors, and telescopes turn his mind inside out, grab hold of him and pull him down, down, down. Sleep had become his only way out of worry.

But not for long.

A noise woke him—a snuffling noise. Rustling. It took a moment for him to remember that he was not in his tent but out on his own in the woods. And there was someone or something in the dark—

nearby. Did other people camp in the woods? Homeless people, maybe?

Jack's breathing slowed, at times stopped altogether. Buried in the sleeping bag, he didn't dare pop his head out. He wished, oh how he wished, he had his tent to act as a barrier. He thought of rolling over and flattening himself against the ground—it seemed as if he would be less vulnerable, more capable of springing up and running, in that position—but he couldn't risk being heard.

Whatever it was made a clicking noise followed by a low rumbling, and Jack thought he'd die of a heart attack before he was discovered. Should he continue to play dead or run? If it was a man or a bear, it was likely he'd be chased. He remained frozen.

It was coming closer, definitely closer. If it was an animal—and, from the snorting sounds, Jack was now pretty certain it was—it no doubt smelled him. What could be in these woods? Bear, moose, coyote. Jack didn't think a moose would intentionally hurt a boy, at least not one stretched out on the ground, but he was definitely less certain about bears and coyotes. Or wolves. He'd forgotten about wolves.

His flashlight was in his backpack. What would happen if he shone a light in the eyes of a wild animal? Would light frighten it away? Anger it? Jack supposed it would depend on the type of animal. He uncurled his fingers, testing their ability to reach for his backpack. To grasp. Why hadn't he thought to tuck the flashlight into his sleeping bag with him?

Scooting up in the sleeping bag in slow, carefully measured increments, Jack reached for his backpack, stretching out his whole arm. But just as his fingers grazed the fabric of the strap, the backpack jerked away.

Robbed. He was being robbed! Whoever it was knew he was here on the ground (had he been seen going into the woods?), knew he had a backpack, knew it and wanted it.

Dang it! He'd already lost a mother and a phone. He couldn't afford to lose anything else. He sat up and yelled, "Hey!"

Yelled at the thief, yelled at the . . . at the *raccoons* who had confiscated his cheese, leaving his backpack on the ground, and were now scrambling away in the bright moonlight.

He didn't know whether to laugh or cry. It wasn't a man or a bear. Just some silly raccoons.

But his cheese. His last bit of food. He could have sworn his stomach growled in protest. Growled at the thought of not eating again, of having no food and too little money to purchase more.

Seven

African elephants have two lobes on the tips of their trunks (Asian elephants have only one), which zoologists refer to as fingers. These fingers are quite flexible and can grasp objects as small as seeds.

It was barely light when he woke, and he was freezing. No way was the earth's center a ball of fire. At this moment, Jack was certain that the core was an ice cube and that it was sending frozen daggers to its surface. He pulled on his Windbreaker, hoping it could stop the cold from penetrating, but it wasn't nearly enough.

So he got up. He rolled up his sleeping bag, put on his backpack, and headed into town.

First line of order was breakfast. Fifty-three cents wouldn't even buy something on the McDonald's

Dollar Menu, a menu he knew by heart. He'd have to find a grocery store. And even then, what would a handful of change buy? Cereal bars were a lot more than this. Were doughnuts? He wasn't sure, but, looking down, he came up with a solution: soda cans and bottles.

He'd seen *ME* next to *MA* on cans all his life, so he was pretty sure that in Maine, just like in Massachusetts, they were returnable. That meant he could get five cents for every drink container he took to the store. He picked up the Diet Coke can at his feet. It was crushed and had been on the side of the road for so long, the label was fading away, but he hoped they'd take it anyway.

On Mount Desert Street, he found a couple of plastic bottles. Fifteen cents in bottle returns gave him sixty-eight cents in all. He hoped to find enough drink containers to bring him to a dollar.

He had his head down, searching, when he nearly bumped into an old man wearing a plaid hunting jacket.

"Look out, son," the man said, not unkindly.

"Sorry!" Jack blurted. "Hey, could you tell me where the nearest grocery store is?"

The man stopped and studied Jack. "You're industrious this morning, aren't you? Go down Roberts Avenue," he said, pointing to the side street next to an inn that looked like a wedding cake. "When you get to the end, turn left."

Roberts Avenue had several houses with signs out front, bed-and-breakfast places. His mother was always telling him how much she loved B&Bs— how the rooms were all different and old-fashioned. "It's like going back in time, Jack," she'd say. "You can imagine that you're someone else altogether."

Jack had never wanted to stay in these places, which looked (at least on the Internet) more like fussy homes than hotels. Besides, they never had swimming pools or cable TV, and those were the best things about traveling.

But . . . maybe? Maybe his mother had walked down this very street, and the pull of puffy bedding, lacy curtains, and not being Becky Martel for a while had been too strong to resist. He stood on the sidewalk and tried to imagine which of these places would call to her: The Maples Inn? Canterbury Cottage? Aysgarth Station? He had no idea what an aysgarth was, or why they'd call a house a station, but he bet his mom would pick that one. It had the most unique name, and his mother was drawn to anything that promised a story.

Jack decided his search would start there. He left his backpack, the two bottles, and the can on the lawn of the B&B, behind a little picket fence, and then bravely walked inside.

No one was in the entryway, so he rang a little bell. A woman popped her head out from around a doorway.

"Is there a Becky Martel staying here?" he asked.

"No, I don't think so," she said, but she didn't seem sure. She wandered over to a book and put her glasses on to check. "No, we don't have a Martel. . . . Does she go by her own name?"

The question startled Jack. Was she asking if his mother might have registered under a different name? Which seemed possible, what with her wanting to feel like someone else and all.

"I mean," said the woman, seeming to read Jack's confusion, "does she have a different name from her husband?"

"Oh. She doesn't have a husband," Jack said,

perhaps a little too quickly. And then, feeling as if he needed to say more, he added: "She's my aunt, and she's coming for a stay on the island, but she must be at another B and B."

The woman nodded but looked at him more carefully now.

He tied the clothing around his waist tighter, said "Thanks anyway!" and bolted out the door.

He threw on his backpack and was ready to run to the next street over, when he realized that his can and two bottles were missing. Who would have taken them? Someone else as hungry as he was at this moment?

"Threw them in the recycling bin," said a man coming around the corner with a rake in his hand. "It was good of you to pick them up."

No! Should he ask for them back?

The man leaned his rake against the porch and went into the B&B.

As much as he wanted to run from the place before the lady inside spotted him again, he couldn't bear the thought of leaving the can and bottles behind. *Maybe,* Jack thought, *the bin is out back— maybe in a shed.* He could find it and get his can and bottles back himself. Behind the B&B was a hinged wooden box about the height of a trash can, and he guessed it might hold recyclables. After making sure no one was watching, he carefully lifted the lid. If the man appeared again, he could say he was just getting his own bottles back.

Sure enough, there they were, on top of a bunch of other soda cans, wine bottles, and even big juice containers. He pulled his can and the two plastic bottles off the top while he calculated the worth of the cans and bottles below.

They wouldn't mind, would they, if he took a couple? Sure, they were worth money, but the man had just taken *his,* hadn't he? And he hadn't thought a thing of it, which probably meant he was planning to recycle these cans and bottles, not redeem them.

What could he put them in? Jack looked under the lid of a second barrel. It was filled with garbage. He spied the handle of a plastic shopping bag and pulled it free. Then he filled the bag with bottles and cans, tallying up nearly two dollars' worth, trying to shut up the voice in his head that whispered, *You're stealing, you know.*

Suddenly, something came flying toward him,

and the heavy top of the box came crashing down on Jack's right hand. He didn't scream, for fear of being caught, but tears jabbed his eyes as he pulled his hand free. It was his pinky, the pinky on his right hand. His pinky was killing him.

He stared at the black-and-white cat that was now perched on top of the box. Its tail twitched as it stared at Jack. Was this a guard cat? Was it protecting the property?

Frozen there, holding his hand, Jack recognized a familiar scent coming from the kitchen. Bacon. One of his favorite things. His stomach called out, reminding him that he needed breakfast. No way was he going to get crispy bacon at the grocery store, but he had to get something. He hadn't really eaten since the picnic yesterday, and, between the hunger pangs and the throbbing in his pinky, he was in no condition to go searching for his mom.

He moved back toward the bin slowly, expecting the cat to hiss or jump at him. Sure enough, the cat crouched, giving only a moment's warning before it leaped into the air.

Thankfully, it didn't leap at Jack but away from him.

Jack quickly lifted the wooden cover, grabbed his nearly full plastic bag with his good hand, and ran down the road toward the grocery store.

Eight

*Even the elephant carries but a small trunk on
his journeys. The perfection of traveling
is to travel without baggage.*
— HENRY DAVID THOREAU

First stop in the supermarket was the bottle-and-can machine, where he made one dollar and ninety cents. Next stop: freezer section. Jack had to get some relief for his hand. Behind a glass door, he found the frozen peas, his mom's ice pack of choice, and plunged his hand deep inside mounds of crunchy bags. Fortunately, it was still fairly early, and most of the shoppers were more interested in coffee than frozen vegetables. He left his hand in as long as he could stand the cold and then pulled it out.

It helped, but he'd hardly made it to the frozen pizza before his pinky started throbbing again, so he slid it into another freezer case. This was how Jack moved up and down the aisles: clinging to frozen orange juice, wrapping his fingers around pints of ice cream. Even yogurt cups, which were not frozen but cool to the touch, provided relief.

He considered spending his money on a bag of ice, or even on some Advil, but knew that the ocean was close by and that he'd be able to give his finger a long soak if the pain didn't go away soon. Instead, he chose trail mix and a bottle of water. The two items had taken all but twenty cents of his money. Sure, there was a water fountain in the store, but he was, once again, really thirsty. He figured he could keep the bottle and fill it up in restrooms, making this the very last time he would have to purchase a drink. As for the trail mix, he'd be careful this time, eating only small amounts as needed.

Easier said than done, he thought as he devoured his first handful, sitting on a sunny wooden bench he'd found sandwiched between the shopping carts and a bike rack, right around the corner from the entrance to the store. He looked out at the parking lot and made himself eat one peanut, one cranberry, and one sunflower seed at a time. Only when he'd chewed what he had in his mouth completely did he allow himself to put his hand back in the bag.

But his hunger was insatiable. And eating took his mind off his finger.

I'll find more bottles and cans, he told himself as he tilted the bag and poured the last remaining seeds into his mouth. *Or better yet, I'll find Mom.*

He hadn't asked anyone in the supermarket if they'd seen his mom; the store was much bigger than he'd imagined, just like the island. Asking seemed silly—futile. Instead, he'd search for his mother the way he searched for information on anything at all back home: he'd find a computer, Google his mother's name, and see what came up—an article mentioning an accident, say. He just needed to find a computer.

The library! he suddenly thought. He could go to the library he'd passed the night before. Infused with new energy, Jack backtracked in that direction, avoiding Roberts Avenue, where he'd stolen the cans and bottles.

Another thought struck him. He could leave

a message for his mom online! He'd write it on her YouPage. Tell her that he was in Bar Harbor. Maybe he'd even set a time and place to meet! It was such an obvious solution to the no-cell-phone problem. Why hadn't he thought of it before?

Sure, she was probably a little crazed at the moment and might not have access to a computer, but who knew? Once when she and Jack were coming home from the Intown Inn, his mom had stopped at the library and rushed to the computers, where she researched everything she could find about grapefruit. At the time, her obsession was kind of embarrassing: she'd kept yelling out little unknown facts: "Jackie, did you know that a grapefruit is a cross between an orange and a pummelo? Have you ever eaten a pummelo?" But today the memory was a happy one—a hope he could hold on to.

By now he was practically running, but the sight of the library up ahead took all the air out of him, like a sucker punch.

It was closed.

Of course. It was Labor Day. All libraries closed on Labor Day. How could he have been so stupid?

Gotten his hopes up like that? He threw his back-pack on the ground. Then picked it up and threw it down again. And again.

"It's Labor Day!" he shouted, as if his mom was right there and could hear him. Labor Day meant not only that all the libraries were closed, but also that his vacation, even if it hadn't officially started, was almost officially over. Tomorrow was supposed to be his first day back at Curley Middle School. His mom had promised they would stop on the way home and buy the supplies he needed: new sneakers, binders, maybe even one of those electronic spell-checkers. No problem, she had said. Everything would be cheaper in Maine.

This time he threw his backpack at a tree, but the strap caught on his pinky finger. The pain was excruciating.

He sat down on the grass and held his hand against his belly.

He hated to accept it, but his pinky was probably broken. He had broken a toe once—banged it at the swimming pool near where his best friend, Nina, lived. As he'd hobbled to the doctor's office, Jack's mom had told him elephant jokes.

"Who does an elephant call when he breaks his toe?"

"Who?"

"The tow truck."

That joke was so bad, Mom had probably made it up.

Jack closed his eyes and pictured a herd of elephants on the savanna. Walking in a long line or playing at a water hole. Why hadn't he been born an elephant? He pictured himself playing with other elephants, spraying them with water from his trunk.

But he wasn't an elephant, and he was not going to find his mother by lying on the lawn of the Jesup Memorial Library.

Dragging himself back to the town center, Jack recalled that Bar Harbor had lots of the types of shops and restaurants his mother would like. Which again made him hopeful; it would be like her to get waylaid in a place that had so many unusual things to see: tourmaline jewels, hand-painted sea chests, blueberry syrup. He might just walk into a shop and see her there.

Jack knew that it wasn't supposed to be this way. That a mother wasn't supposed to go off without telling her kid . . . and that her kid wasn't supposed to be able to walk into a store and find her there coincidentally. He wished that things were different. That he could be the one hanging out in a store and that his mom would be the one to pop in and say, "What are you doing in here, Jack? I've been looking all over for you!"

Once, Nina had asked him why he was alone so much, and he had tried to tell her—tell her about his mom's pinwheel times. How sometimes the air felt so still to her, like there wasn't any oxygen or breezes to be found. These times made his mom so prickly, she could hardly sit still. And she crabbed a lot. So sometimes she stayed away because she didn't think it was fair that she was being mean.

But then the wind would come, the air would be light, and she could, well, float! And even though the world looked the same to *him,* his mom said she could see things, magical things: lit pathways in the sky, a spider web that connected all living things. "You are connected to the elephants, Jack," she'd say. Once, during a spinning time, she'd brought home every single flavor of ice cream the store had, and they'd done a taste test. (Ben and Jerry's Chunky Monkey was the best.)

Another time, she kept asking him, "What is the rarest color?" Jack had done a Google search, but he could only find answers to questions like, *What is the rarest eye color?* (green), and, *What is the rarest color of geckos?* (no one agrees). So he and his mother went to OfficeMax (where there would be lots and lots of little items) and began tallying the number of times they saw each color. The noncolors—black, white, and gray—were everywhere. Fuchsia and lime green were kind of rare, but the rarest of all was a brownish purple his mother named *sunken treasure.* From then on, they had searched for objects that were this rare color— more red than blue, more brown than red. It was weird: Once he knew this color existed, he *yearned* for it. And he felt stupidly happy when he saw it somewhere—in the bark of a tree, or in a picture in his social studies book.

One day, he'd come home from school and there was a bill from a foreign country sitting on his bed—he couldn't remember where the bill was from, but he knew that the country wasn't the part that mattered. It was the color. The bill was sunken treasure. Only one other person in the whole world would know that.

But Nina had said, "Why did she just leave the money on your bed? Why didn't she give it to you herself? Why does she have to stay away from the apartment so much?" And because she didn't understand, Jack didn't tell her any more.

Nine

A forest elephant that had torn his trunk while freeing himself from a trap was in too much pain to feed himself. So he walked right up to an African savanna elephant in Kenya's Masai Mara National Reserve and put his trunk in the other elephant's mouth. The African elephant understood: he immediately ripped up an acacia tree and fed it to his new acquaintance.

As Jack walked up and down Main Street in Bar Harbor, he read the signs: THE ACADIA SHOP, COOL AS A MOOSE, BEN AND BILL'S CHOCOLATE EMPORIUM. Outside Ben and Bill's was a tall wooden lobster holding a triple-decker ice-cream cone in its claw. Two little kids were sitting in its lap. He knew his mother would love this place.

It was still fairly early in the morning, but already the shop was busy. Although there were chocolates of every kind, and although cotton candy hung from the chocolate racks, it was the ice cream that was in demand. It seemed that most of the customers in line were interested in trying the lobster ice cream, and the guy behind the counter was happy to give them a taste on tiny spoons. Jack hadn't noticed his hunger before he walked into the shop, but now that he smelled the chocolate and saw all the ice cream and gelato flavors, he felt ravenous. How many tastes could he have? And what would happen if he tasted the ice cream but didn't order anything?

If he could sample only one flavor, he didn't want to waste it on something like lobster ice cream—what if he didn't like it? Would the guy think it was strange if he tasted something he knew he'd love? Could he taste Chocolate Peanut-Butter Cookie Dough?

He bravely asked. Sure enough, the guy scooped it out without hesitation.

Jack held the wooden spoon in his mouth and simply let the ice cream melt off, trying to savor every sweet drop. He pressed the bit of cookie dough to the roof of his mouth and slowly chewed on a chocolate chip. Surely this way he'd feel like he'd eaten a whole cup.

But the little sample disappeared in seconds.

Did he dare ask for another?

"Could I taste Chewy Gooey?"

Again, he got a taste. Wow.

"May I help you?" the scooper asked a woman standing next to him.

"Oh," said the woman. "This young man was here before me. Go ahead and take his order first."

The scooper looked at Jack. "What'll it be?"

Jack hadn't chosen another flavor to sample, and he was clearly expected to get on with ordering an ice-cream cone. What should he do?

He looked from the woman to the guy. "It's OK," he said. "I haven't made up my mind."

The woman ordered butter-pecan ice cream. Jack flew out the door without even asking the guy if he'd seen his mother. But Bar Harbor was so crowded, so busy, that even if the guy had seen her, would he have remembered?

Only if she's flying high, he thought, then quickly pushed the thought away.

Jack walked up and down the sidewalk, dipping into stores, for much of the morning. In every shop he entered, he saw something that would have caught his mother's interest: lobster salt-and-pepper shakers, a snow globe with a giant seagull looming over a sailboat, moose pajama pants. There were so many people (every now and then someone with blond hair would momentarily make his heart beat faster), and so many treasures his mom would love, he felt she *had* to be close by. So convinced was he that he visited several stores two or three times.

He had just decided to try looking at the village green, when he passed a bald guy who was wearing a *Geddy's* T-shirt. His mom had that shirt! She had worn it so many times you could hardly read the name. He'd never asked her what it meant, but now it felt like this guy was walking around with a piece of his mother, a piece of code.

"Hey!" Jack yelled at the guy's back. To his surprise, the man turned around. "What's Geddy's?"

"A bar — and a restaurant," the man answered. "It's right down there," he said, pointing toward the water.

Had his mom mentioned it when they put Bar Harbor on the list of things to see? Probably. But she had talked of so many places in Maine, Jack had begun to let some of them roll over his ears.

Especially when she'd ignored the one thing he really wanted to do.

He walked in the direction in which the man had pointed. Main Street dipped down a hill. On the right-hand side of the hill was a park with an amazing view of the ocean. There were all kinds of boats docked in the harbor: lobster boats, speed-boats, even an enormous cruise ship. And a tall ship, the type of ship Jack had seen tucked inside a bottle. This ship had flags at the top of its four masts. Across the street from the park were more shops and restaurants, and sure enough, there was a sign that read MEET ME AT GEDDY'S.

This felt like such a lucky break. Surely, if his mom had come into Bar Harbor, she had gone there.

With one foot on the blue-carpeted steps that led up to the restaurant, Jack waited for a family to go in ahead of him. The hostess gathered menus and motioned for the family to follow her, and when they'd all turned away, Jack slipped past the hostess stand and headed up to the oval bar that stood smack in the center of a very long room.

He slid in between two stools, waiting to get the attention of the bartender, a young guy who reminded Jack of the college kids who worked at the Intown Inn during the summer. He'd known as soon as he approached the bar that his mother wasn't there. Maybe it was the quiet, or the seeming dimness that had nothing at all to do with the red lights that glowed above the bar. He found himself staring at a baseball game on one of the four TVs until disappointment let go of his chest and he could breathe regularly again. He made himself look around to confirm what his heart already knew.

There was a young couple seated at one end of the bar, sharing a Red Bull, and a bookish woman typing on her laptop at the other. Every so often, she'd pause and take a bite of her salad. And there was a large, bearded man sitting close to where Jack was standing, holding a soda between both hands.

"Might as well sit up here," said the bearded man, patting the stool beside him. "He's going to be a while."

The bartender was filling a large drink order for a waitress with long eyelashes, whose eyes opened and closed in a way that kind of reminded Jack of a llama. The bartender moved from making several green drinks with salt around the rim of the glasses to blending chocolaty drinks with whipped cream on top.

Jack slid up onto the stool and stared at the walls of the restaurant as if he'd never been in a bar that was covered with signs and license plates and other random junk like oars and stuff before. Truth was, he and his mom had been in lots of bars exactly like this one. Many a night, he'd stared at random words on the wall—words like *To become old and wise, one must first be young and stupid*—and wondered when they could finally go home. What was it about this place that made it so special to his mom?

The man next to him gave his shoulder a nudge. The bartender was waiting.

"Oh. Could I have a glass of water?" Jack asked.

"Sure," said the bartender. "What happened to your hand?"

Jack looked down at his hand, resting on the edge of the shiny copper bar. He'd gotten so used to the steady pulsing of his finger that he'd almost forgotten about his injury. But that one finger was clearly larger than the rest, and bent at a slightly odd angle. It was black-and-blue between the knuckles.

"Looks broken," said his neighbor, taking another sip of his soda.

"You should get that checked," said the bartender, scooping ice into a glass.

"Nah," said the bearded guy. "I've broken a finger plenty of times playing football. Ice it and splint it. It'll heal fine. Here," he said, motioning to the bartender. "Fill one of those rags with ice."

The bartender took a cloth, filled it with ice, and placed it on Jack's finger.

The bearded guy nodded. "What's your name?"

"Jack."

"No way," said the guy. "Jack's my name! Do they call you Jackie?"

"Just Mo—my mother. Sometimes." Jack turned to the bartender. "Have you seen a woman in here? With short blond hair and blue eyes? She's kind of skinny and she wears hoop earrings."

The other Jack—Big Jack—laughed. "You're going to have to do better than that, kid. You're describing one-quarter of America."

"Does she have a tattoo?" asked the bartender. "A tiny one, right here?" He pointed to the soft place between his forefinger and his thumb.

Jack nodded. She had a tattoo. A tiny orchid. The bartender had seen his mother! He remembered her! "When was she here?" he asked breathlessly.

"Yesterday . . . no, the day before. Saturday morning."

Two whole days ago! Different emotions rushed to be first in line. Jack took a sip of water, pushing them all back, making them wait.

"Did she stay long?" Jack asked.

"She was talking to someone," the bartender said. "Guy who works for Hinckley."

"Sails yachts," Big Jack said. "I know who you're talkin' about now. She was a live wire. She your mom?"

Jack knew that if he said yes, they'd be more careful about the details they shared. "She's someone I met," he said.

"I see," said Big Jack. "Hey, Gary, give me that pencil over there. And, Laurie"—he grabbed the

attention of a pretty waitress as she walked by—
"you got a first-aid kit back there?"

"I don't know. Maybe."

"Go get it for me, please," said Big Jack.

He must spend a lot of time here, thought Jack, moving his finger out from under the ice for a moment.

"Well, she was here through lunch," said the bartender. "The guy she was talking to was getting ready to go off on a charter."

"What's that?" asked Jack.

"He's going to sail someone's boat to warmer waters, now that the season's over here," said Big Jack.

"Warmer like Boston?" asked Jack.

The two men laughed like that was the funniest thing they'd ever heard. "Warmer like the Bahamas," said the bartender.

Jack stopped breathing, which must have blocked oxygen from going to his head. He felt dizzy, like he might faint.

Just then, the waitress—*Laurie,* Jack thought, trying not to think about anything else other than her name—put a little plastic box on the bar.

"Mudo," said Big Jack.

Jack looked up. *"Mudo?"*

"Means 'thank you' in Ewe," said Big Jack, "which is what they speak in parts of Ghana, in Africa."

"Have you been there?" asked Jack. He'd heard of Ghana. They had lots of African-elephant conservation programs there. It seemed like a lucky sign.

"A long time ago," Big Jack said as he opened the first-aid kit and pulled out some gauze and a roll of tape. He measured the pencil against Jack's pinky and broke the pencil in two. Then he carefully wrapped Jack's pinky with gauze and tape, using the pencil as a splint. It didn't hurt a bit. Or if it had, Jack hadn't noticed.

"Don't worry," said Big Jack. "This is sort of my job."

"Are you a doctor?"

"No. I help kids that need help. So, where'd you meet this woman?" asked Big Jack.

"Seawall Campground," said Jack. Lying was getting easier and easier. "She thought she might meet me here. She has something for me."

"Yeah?" said Big Jack. His eyes told Jack he didn't believe him.

"Well, I think you're out of luck," said the bartender. "I'd say she's on her way to tropical beaches."

Jack put his glass to his lips and attempted to finish his water, but his throat was blocked. His mother, on a boat. *Bahamas.* He slid off the stool.

"How about a cheeseburger?" asked Big Jack. "On me?"

Jack knew he should take this man up on the offer, knew he should get something to eat and maybe figure out a way to explain his predicament, but he couldn't. He was about to lose it. All it would take was one more question, one more kind look, and Jack would spill everything. He couldn't risk it. He had to think. He had to get air.

"I can't. I've got to get going. Thanks anyway," said Jack. He couldn't even look up at Big Jack. "And thanks for fixing my finger!" he called as he turned and ran out of the restaurant, back into the glaring sunlight.

The street was overflowing with couples and families enjoying their last day here on the island. Only none of them *was* an island. They had each other—holding hands, laughing, pointing things out to one another. Jack had no one. Not his mother, who was probably on her way to the Bahamas; not his grandmother, who wanted to steal him away from his mother; not even his one and only friend, Nina, who refused to understand. No one. He was in a bustling, crowded place, and he was entirely alone.

At least he wasn't hungry anymore. In fact, he was pretty sure that if he ate anything right now, he'd throw up. To get away from the odor of a nearby restaurant with wide-open windows, Jack ducked into Sherman's, a book- and gift shop. The store was packed with tourists, and twice he bumped into someone with his stuffed backpack. He couldn't help it. His eyes were darting from face to face, searching for his mom, willing her to be here, willing the bartender to be wrong.

His mom would love this place: books and tchotchkes. He meandered through the crowd to the nonfiction section. He loved to read. In fact, it was one reason why being alone in the apartment didn't freak him out. He could usually lose himself in a book or in comics in a way he couldn't when he was watching TV or playing video games.

There were no books about elephants, only ones about Maine animals, so he wandered over to the fiction section. There, he picked up a book called *Trouble*—he was sure having enough of that—but the words swam before his eyes. He snapped it shut and placed it back on the shelf.

From the book section, he squeezed his way toward the shelves that held toys. Mostly, they were the kinds of toys that keep kids busy during long car trips—kids like him, who didn't have DVD players. He turned his eyes away from the mechanical puzzles and the Mad Libs, saw a rack of plastic animals, and smiled. These were the types of toys he had liked best when he was younger.

He wrapped the fingers of his left hand around the neck of a plastic giraffe—so smooth to the touch. If he'd been alone in the store, he would have smelled the plastic. He searched for an elephant.

He thought he saw one in the corner of the rack, but it was a rhino. Jack held the rhino for a moment before putting it back. He remembered a story he'd read—a *true* story—about a mother elephant who tried to rescue a baby rhinoceros who was stuck in mud. The elephant was using her trunk to rock the baby loose, but the mother rhino didn't understand. She thought the elephant was threatening her baby, and she charged, forcing the elephant to back away. The mama elephant would wait awhile and then go back and try to free the calf. She was charged time and time again, maimed, even—rhinos can be really fierce—but the elephant wouldn't give up. She wouldn't leave that baby to die.

Jack searched madly for an elephant and finally found one, a small one, walking on tiptoes the way elephants do. Even though it was a toy, he knew it was an African elephant: the highest point was not its shoulder but the center of its back. Its trunk was pointed up—a symbol of good luck, his art teacher had told him once when she'd examined his drawings. Jack held the baby elephant in both hands. Its wrinkled trunk lay against his splintered finger.

"May I help you?" asked a woman suddenly standing at his side.

"How much is this elephant?" he asked, knowing full well the cost was more than the coins he had in his pocket.

"I think the small size is two-fifty," she said. "But I can check if you want."

"That'd be great," he said. Maybe they'd hold it for him.

As the woman walked away to check the price, Jack calculated the number of bottles he would have to find to purchase this elephant, remembering that there'd be tax. More than fifty. Even if he dug in trash cans, it was unlikely he'd be able to collect that many, and have money left over for food, too. Besides, he should probably be thinking about saving up for a bus ticket or something.

The elephant seemed to smile at him. He searched the rack for other elephants, but there were none. Just this baby.

A lone one. Like him.

Jack's thoughts spun. The elephant was so small, and the store was so crowded. . . .

He thought of his mother, thought of her leaving him here on an island, thought of her laughing and spinning and seeing magical things with some guy on a sailboat. . . .

He did it.

He slipped the elephant into his pocket and ran toward the door.

"Hey!" the woman yelled. "Stop!"

He didn't stop. He pushed his way through hordes of tourists and out the door.

"Jack!" he heard. The voice was a deep bellow. It must be Big Jack from the restaurant. He kept running.

Then he heard his name again. This time, a woman's voice: "Jack!"

Mom? He looked over his shoulder.

But no. It was just the woman from the store. Standing next to her was Big Jack, hunched over from running.

Jack kept going, shouts of "Get back here!" fading behind him.

Ten

*Farmers in Africa plant hot chili peppers
around their crops to keep elephants away.*

Jack ran straight out of town. Not only had he stolen something (more than one thing, if you counted the cans and bottles he'd taken from the B&B), but people *knew* he had stolen something, and they knew his name. He was only a sighting away from being caught.

He ran away from the crowded sidewalks, past the gazebo on the village green, down sidewalkless, winding island streets for about twenty minutes, until he came to a dirt road. Would they search for him down there? Not likely. After gulping down the entire contents of his water bottle, he followed the rutty road to a single farmhouse surrounded by fields.

There didn't seem to be much activity at the house. No cars in the driveway, no tractor in the distance. An old black-and-white dog came out of the barn and ambled up to him, like it was his regular job to greet guests and be petted. Didn't even bother to bark.

"Hello?" Jack called, having no idea what he would say if someone appeared. But no one responded.

Jack noticed the house was a lot like this dog: nice but worn down. Kind of tilted in some places and bulging in others. After a few pats, the dog strolled back into the barn. Jack followed him.

At one time there might have been livestock in this barn, cows or sheep, maybe, but not any longer. Now it was being used for storage of old, rusty equipment and gardening tools.

Cool! There was a loft. Ever since his third-grade teacher had read the part in *Charlotte's Web* where Avery and Fern swing from a rope in Mr. Zuckerman's barn, Jack had wanted to look down from a loft. He climbed the wooden ladder cautiously, trying not to put weight on his sore finger.

There were some cushions and some scratchy wool blankets up there, and a wooden box turned over to make a table of sorts. Jack guessed that kids used to play here—maybe even had sleepovers. But it was clear from the look of things that it had been a long time ago. Mouse droppings were everywhere.

Even though Jack was from the city, mouse poop didn't gross him out. Heck, in the city he'd seen rats—and their apartment had plenty of roaches. Mice were nothing at all. Jack shook one of the blankets out and covered the cushions. Then he sat down and tried to imagine that he lived on this farm. That this loft belonged to him. He pulled the elephant out of his pocket and placed it on the box where he could see it. It was his now.

He yanked his sleeping bag out of his backpack, and his comic books, too. He'd rest here for a little bit, and then he'd figure out what to do.

It was night when he woke with a start. He'd fallen asleep, and it was pitch-black in the barn. Without his cell phone, he didn't know if it was ten o'clock at night or two o'clock in the morning. He lay there, wondering what he was going to do. What if the bartender had been wrong? What if his mother was looking for him? *Maybe I should go back to the campsite tomorrow,* thought Jack.

But school started tomorrow. *How long will it be,* he wondered, *before the guidance counselor starts looking for me?* Would he just be wasting valuable time by hoping his mother showed up?

"On her way to tropical beaches," the bartender had said.

Round and round went his thoughts, each one feeling momentarily promising . . . and then hopeless. Night sounds — crickets, a truck horn in the distance — grew louder around him. Everything had an opinion.

Jack knew the dog was still down below; he could hear its tags jangling as it scratched itself. *Too bad dogs can't climb ladders,* he thought. He would have liked that old dog stretched out beside him. For a moment, he contemplated getting down from the loft and sleeping with the dog. But the cushions were comfortable, and he still felt so very tired. That's what worry did to Jack, made him incredibly tired— tired the way his mom always was after the spinning times. She'd come home and crawl into bed, close the shades, and pull up the covers, and that's where Jack would find her for days—sometimes even weeks— after a spinning time. Tired like that. He closed his eyes and fell back to sleep.

When he woke again, sunlight was sliding through all the cracks in the walls, giving the barn a sort of comfortable, cozy feeling—until, that is, he remembered that today was the day his vacation was officially over. Then nothing felt comfortable. The cushions were lumpy. His mouth was dry. It felt like mice had made a nest in it while he slept. And he was hungry—boy, was he hungry! He hadn't eaten anything but a bag of trail mix and two tastes of ice cream yesterday.

I'm on a farm, he thought as he left his stuff—all but his empty water bottle, that is—and climbed down the ladder. *There has to be a garden, right?* After all, the barn was full of gardening tools. And if there was a garden, surely there would be a hose for watering the garden. He didn't know which would taste better right now: a big, crunchy carrot or a mouthful of cool, running water. He'd find something to eat, and then he'd figure out a plan.

Not knowing if the farm family had returned, he pushed the barn door open a crack. He and the dog slipped through; then he moved around to the side of the barn where he couldn't be seen from the house. There it was, the garden. He could see a scarecrow in a back field not far from where he stood. Only problem was, he'd have no place to hide while picking; anyone looking out the back window would see him.

He went around front to see if a car had come in during the night. Mist was rising, hovering just above the fields with hay bales, across the road, and not a car in sight. Not on the dirt road that had led him here, not in the driveway, either. Maybe the owners had gone away for the long weekend. Even country people needed a vacation, right?

Jack guessed it would be safe to help himself to a vegetable or two. *Heck,* he thought as he walked around back through the dew-soaked grass to the garden, *the vegetables are just going to go to waste if these people aren't here to pick them.*

A net, held up by tall poles, surrounded the garden (to keep away deer?), but Jack spotted a place where the netting could be untied and the garden entered. He was barely through when he spotted a ripe tomato calling his name. The skin was warm from the morning sun, and he held it to his nose for just a moment before biting into it like it was a big old apple or a juicy plum. Seeds squirted out, dripping down his chin.

He reached for another.

"So. You think you can just help yourself to my tomatoes?"

Jack jumped, using his forearm to wipe the evidence off his chin. He hadn't heard the woman approach. But there she was, not more than a few feet from him, standing crossly in her black rubber boots and straw hat. Glancing around, he noticed sheets on a line on the side of the house opposite the barn. There was a basket on the ground beneath them. She must have been hanging the wash.

Of course she'd seen him.

"S-sorry," he stammered. "The tomato—it's just—"

"Where're you from?" She swatted a fly away from her face.

"I was running down your road. Training." Where did that come from? Jack had never trained for anything in his life, though he had thought about going out for football now that he was going to be in sixth grade this fall.

She was staring at his splinted finger, which was looking pretty dirty already. "Why aren't you in school today?" she asked. "Or is this one of those years when you don't start the day after Labor Day?"

He just nodded, having no idea whether the kids in Maine were back today or not.

"You ate from the pantry row," she said.

"Pantry row?"

"Don't you garden?"

Jack shook his head.

"Well, then, you wouldn't know. We're encouraged to plant one row of vegetables for the food pantry. That way, those in need can have fresh vegetables. Not just Hamburger Helper."

"Sorry," he said again as the woman sized him up.

"Tell you what," she said. "I can't drive any longer. Stubborn son took my car. So I have no way to get these vegetables into town. If you'll pick this row and take 'em up to the pantry, I'll let you bring some home for your family. That way, I'll get my vegetables harvested before the frost, and you'll get more training: heavy lifting," she said, trying not to smile.

No way! Jack thought. He didn't need to be gardening and running errands for some old lady he didn't even know. He had a mother to find. He glanced off into the woods, considered bolting. But his stuff—it was still up in the loft. And what would she do if he ran? Would she know he was lying about living nearby? About school? Would she be suspicious enough to call the police?

He looked down at the garden. There were green beans dangling right next to the ripe tomatoes. The woman did say she'd give him food. . . .

And while he was back in town, he could go back to the library, get online. It was Tuesday; the library would surely be open today.

"It's a deal," he said.

She gave him instructions on how to pick the last of the summer vegetables — green beans, red peppers, cucumbers, tomatoes, zucchini, basil, carrots, and potatoes — and then she went back to hanging clothes. Jack was tempted to eat as he picked, especially the carrots, which didn't look like the ones his mother bought from the store but were palm-size and curled a little, like wiggly goldfish pulled from the ground. He used his fingers to wipe away the dirt on one and glanced at the old woman, who had now moved on to watering her flowers.

She was looking right up at him, as if his guiltiness had called her. Jack went back to picking.

The next time he looked up, the woman was walking toward him. She placed most of the vegetables into a large, netted bag. "Bring these to the pantry," she said, tying the top. "Tell them they're from Mrs. Olson. And tell them I need a box of dried milk — they can spare one."

Jack nodded.

"When you get back, you can take this home with you," she said, tossing the rest of the vegetables into a paper bag, which she set by the front porch.

"Ask your mom to make you a harvest stew. Maybe it'll inspire you to plant some tomatoes next year."

With permission, he filled up his water bottle at the hose and took off.

It wasn't until he had walked for about ten minutes that he realized a tomato wasn't exactly the most filling of breakfasts and that, well, he could just hide this food in the woods and tell the woman he'd delivered it. Or not tell her anything at all— just sneak back and get his stuff from the loft and the bag of vegetables from the front porch.

But what about the dried milk? asked a voice inside his head.

He remembered the woman's half smile. *I was just what-iffing,* he answered. He wasn't going to take these vegetables. He didn't have to steal this time. She was giving him food. No, he was *working* for food.

But boy, was he hungry. Really hungry. Suddenly, something new occurred to him. This food he was carrying? It was for people who couldn't afford to buy food. He couldn't buy food. It was for people like *him*.

He thought about the homeless people that he recognized in Jamaica Plain: the woman who sat outside the Laundromat and sometimes asked passersby to brush her hair, and the man who was dressed in a suit—a ratty suit, but still, he always wore a tie—and offered to write a poem for a dollar. Once, Jack had paid him, and the man had written this:

We all wear bifocals
Some invisible
When looking down, remember to look up
the view might be clearer
And vice versa

How had those people ended up so needy? Were they living comfortably one day and on the street the next?

And now he was one of them. No food and no money to buy it. That being the case, the people at the food pantry probably wouldn't mind if he ate just one carrot. Just one. So he did. One fresh, wiggly carrot.

And, walking along, chomping on that carrot, trying to make it last as long as he could, he realized two more things: one, he had no idea where the food pantry was located, and two, he was heading right back into Bar Harbor—the place where just yesterday he had run from.

Eleven

Elephant bulls leave their mothers and the rest of the cow herd at around twelve years of age and wander solo.

The outside of the Jesup Memorial Library, where Jack knew he could find directions to the food pantry, looked like half a dozen libraries he and his mom had visited: it was a small brick building with large, decorative windows.

He didn't think walking in with a big sack of vegetables was wise—not if he wanted to remain unnoticed—so he hid them to the right of the book-return box, behind some low shrubs. He doubted anyone would notice them.

The inside of the library surprised him. It was elegant, like a mansion—all polished wood and heavy furniture, the kind of fancy furniture that filled his grandmother's house. The ceilings were high—way high—with massive chandeliers. *I must stick out like a sore—Like my sore pinky,* he thought, looking down at the mess of a bandage. It was tattered and covered with dirt from the garden, and so loose he could easily slip it off—which he did, tucking it in his pocket. No use bringing more attention to himself.

There were a few old people in the main room, and one family with little kids heading into the children's room, but no kids his age. Of course not; they were all back in school. But that was OK— he was from Massachusetts, and school might start later there, or heck, his mom could have kept him out of school for their vacation.

He tried to act as cool as possible when he approached the librarian. "Excuse me."

She looked up.

"Hi, I'm visiting from Massachusetts, and I was wondering—"

"Aren't you lucky! Kids in Maine went back to school today."

He smiled and nodded. "Are there — is there a computer I can use?"

She looked as if he'd just presented her with an insurmountable problem. "Well, normally you have to have a letter signed by your parent," she said.

He waited, trusting she'd give in.

"Oh, I don't think it could hurt," she said, moving from the back of the desk to the front. "Follow me. I'll log you on." Jack followed the librarian down the stairs to a small room with more book stacks and three computers. "There isn't room for all our books upstairs, but we can't bear to part with them. We call this room our treasure trove," she said.

Jack glanced at some of the titles that had been considered too precious to let go of while she leaned over and logged him on. When she left, Jack slipped into the chair and typed *Rebecca Martel*. It took him longer than usual because his big, fat pinky kept hitting the wrong keys. He figured that Big Jack and the bartender were right, that his mom was on her way to the Bahamas, but he still wanted to put his mind at ease, to know for sure that she hadn't been hurt or arrested.

He began to read the entries, several of which

he'd seen before. There was a lawyer in Washington, D.C., named Rebecca Martel, and a real-estate broker in Iowa. He skipped ahead a few pages, making sure that her name wasn't in the news. It wasn't, and the muscles in his neck and shoulders relaxed. Then he clicked on his mom's YouPage, wondering if she had access to a computer and, if so, whether was she making entries—or leaving messages on other people's pages? On his page?

He couldn't look while the page was loading. Instead, he glanced over at the woman at the next computer, who was typing with a baby in her lap. A pacifier popped out of the baby's mouth and rolled onto the floor. The mother leaned over, picked up the pacifier, sucked on it herself, and then slid it back into the baby's mouth.

He made himself look at the page. Not a trace of recent activity anywhere.

He clicked on his own YouPage. A message would say so much—that she'd been thinking about him, that she knew he'd be smart enough to get to a computer. It might even tell him what she was thinking or, at the very least, what he should do next.

Nothing. Jack's throat dried up. He took a swig

of water from the bottle he was carrying, hoping he wouldn't get in trouble for drinking in the library.

Maybe it was better that his mom hadn't written. Leaving a note would mean that she wasn't spinning, but was rational and making decisions. Decisions like, *I'll write Jack a note.* Decisions like, *I'm going to leave Jack in Maine.*

Don't be stupid, he said to himself. She wouldn't *decide* that.

It was like the elephant he stole yesterday. Right now, it was sitting on the box back in the barn. He had no intention of leaving it there—that elephant was special. It was like it was meant to belong to him. But something could happen, right? Something could prevent him from going back to get it. Mrs. Olson could discover his things and call the police, who would arrest him when he returned. Or maybe the woman from the gift shop would be standing right there on the sidewalk when he walked out of the library, and she'd grab him. Then Jack would *have* to leave the elephant. These things happened.

Thinking about the elephant, *his* elephant, made him feel anxious. He wished he had put it in his pocket when he woke up.

A message screen popped up on his YouPage. It was Nina!

Nina: How come ur not in school?
Jack: How come UR not in school?
Nina: I am! I'm hanging out in the computer lab.
Jack: Bingham will kill u if he sees u on UPage
Nina: First day of school. He'll go easy. Answer my question.
Jack: Long story
Nina: Once upon a time . . .

Jack laughed. He was always saying *long story*, and she was always getting him to talk. But this time he didn't know what to say. He began tentatively.

Jack: We decided to stay awhile longer
Nina: Your mom's letting u skip again?
Jack: Yeah, u know her
Nina: So everything's OK?

More than anything, he wished he could tell Nina—could get her to help him figure things out.

But he couldn't tell anyone this time. Not even his best friend.

Jack: Course
Nina: Hey! Did you see the elephant?

Nina had been with Jack when he discovered that there was actually an elephant in Maine—an elephant right off the Maine Pike, the road they'd taken north. The elephant's name was Lydia. It was what he and his mother had argued about.

Jack: Nah. My mom wasn't feeling well—

That summed up a lot, and was probably true.

Nina: Is your mom with you now?
Jack: Affirmative
Nina: She isn't, is she?
Jack: Gotta run. TTYS

Jack closed the screen before Nina could say anything else.

Thinking of her hanging out in the computer

lab just frustrated him more. He typed in the Curley Middle School address and read the welcome-back message from his principal and a note about the upcoming Fall Fling. The Fling was a blast last year, and he wanted to be back there, back there with Nina. At least at home, he knew how to do things. He knew if he needed to, he could go over to Nina's house for dinner. Or he could walk to Ten Tables restaurant, where the owner was a friend of his mother's. There he'd be pulled into the kitchen and fed something yummy. Here in Bar Harbor, there was no one to help him.

Another woman came into the room. She walked behind Jack and sat at a computer at the far end of the table. The mom next to him greeted her. "Hey there. Was work crazy this weekend?"

"You know it! You wouldn't believe what happened yesterday," said the woman.

Jack recognized that voice—it was the woman from Sherman's! The one who had seen him steal the elephant! The one who knew his name.

Jack huddled closer to the computer, turning his back toward both women. "I'm glad summer is over," the woman continued. "I'm tired of the crowds."

He held his breath. Would she mention a boy who had shoplifted? And if she did, would the mother suddenly look over, wonder who this kid was, sitting here in the middle of a Tuesday morning?

Jack wondered if he should try to sneak out another way. Was there another way? Or maybe he should move back into the book stacks until the woman left.

"I'm so tired of the restaurant business," said the woman.

Restaurant? Jack got up the courage to look at the woman and let out a long breath. She wasn't the woman from Sherman's. She was the waitress from Geddy's. Laurie.

So it wasn't so close a call after all. But he knew one thing. He'd go crazy if he stayed in Bar Harbor.

He searched for directions from Bar Harbor to Jamaica Plain and pulled down the arrow to walking time. According to the site, it would take him three days and thirteen hours to walk home. Of course, he'd have to stop and sleep. But still, he could probably be home in a week. He had his sleeping bag. Who knew—maybe he would even get brave enough to hitchhike.

But wait! The Island Explorer! The free bus didn't just go around the island. It went over to the mainland, too. Jack typed in *island explorer,* and sure enough, there was a bus leaving the village green for Trenton every half hour. Trenton was the town just on the other side of the bridge, but it was a start. He'd bring Mrs. Olson her milk, collect his things, and be on the mainland by tonight.

He searched for *food pantry bar harbor,* and a link popped right up. It was in the basement of the YWCA—and it was only two doors down! He remembered passing the sign.

He thanked the librarian, grabbed the vegetables, and went next door. To access the food pantry, he had to go around to the back of the brick YWCA building. There were discarded screens and a Dumpster back there, but there was also a little parking lot, making it easier, Jack figured, for people to pick up food without feeling like everyone in the whole world knew they needed it.

According to the website, Tuesday morning was one of the few days that the pantry was open, and there were lots of older people and mothers with little children waiting to sign in. When it was Jack's turn, he explained that the vegetables were from Mrs. Olson and that she needed powdered milk.

"She'll need lots more than that," said the man, pulling out the vegetables and placing them in plastic bins, "now that the growing season is over. Come on," he said. "We'll refill her bag."

Jack followed the man around as he filled the bag with pancake mix and syrup, spaghetti, toilet paper, and canned tuna, turkey, and salmon.

"We won't need to give her canned vegetables; she'll have her own. But we'll throw in some of this fruit cocktail."

Jack knew he'd be tempted to take a can of something from Mrs. Olson's bag on his walk back to her farm, but he wouldn't let himself do that. The pantry was counting on her having this food. And who knew how long this food had to last her? He was beginning to see the spiderweb that his mother was talking about: Mrs. Olson used her garden to connect to the food pantry, and now he was one of the strands that helped make that web stronger.

He wished there was a way he could ask for food for himself. But even food pantries had their rules. He'd watched people fill out forms or sign in. The pantry staff would have to know something about him. He couldn't give them facts, and he didn't think he was clever enough to lie—not to fool these people. An eleven-year-old kid coming in for food? That was just the sort of thing that would put them on his trail.

But maybe he could suggest something extra. Something they wouldn't have put in the bag otherwise. Something for him.

"There," said the guy, putting the dried milk on top.

"Hey," said Jack, the words practically catching in his throat. "Do you think she would like some cereal bars?"

The man smiled. "Well," he said, "I wouldn't have thought . . . but who knows?"

Jack began to reach for his favorite strawberry brand.

"But let's choose those over there. They're more nutritious."

The day had grown hot—or at least it seemed so to Jack, who was carrying an incredibly heavy bag back to Mrs. Olson's farm. The cans were forever rolling around in the bag, shifting the weight from one side to the other. Twice, the netted bag had caught on his broken finger, causing pain to pulse right up through his arm. He had to stop every five minutes or so to rest. He wished Mrs. Olson had given him a wheelbarrow or something. He was tempted to break into the cereal bars, but, knowing how long the trip back home would take him, he vowed to be careful with food. He would wait until he was back at the farm.

He couldn't wait to see Mrs. Olson's face when he gave her this bag. He felt like Santa delivering a sack of presents. But before going to her door, he snuck into the barn. He dropped the bag and grabbed the box of cereal bars, then climbed into the loft. There he devoured one bar in four bites. A few crumbs remained in the package. He remembered an elephant his mom once told him about, who was captive but each day put aside a little of his grain for a mouse to eat. Jack made a little mound with the crumbs on the spot where he had slept.

He dumped the five remaining bars into his backpack, hid the cardboard box under the wooden table, and placed the toy elephant securely in his pocket.

On Mrs. Olson's doorstep was his bag of vegetables, with a little note that said *Thank you*. Jack rang her doorbell, eager to show her all he had brought, but she didn't answer. Maybe she wasn't home, but he suspected otherwise. He suspected it was something else that kept her from opening the door. A kind of pride, maybe.

Jack picked up his vegetables, threw on his backpack, and started his 248-mile walk home.

Twelve

Riddle: How do you know if an elephant is hiding in your refrigerator?
Answer: There are footprints in the butter.

As the bus traveled to the mainland, Jack read the schedule and tried to decide on the best place to get off. The farthest point the bus traveled to was the IGA in Trenton. He was pretty sure the IGA was a supermarket; he and his mother had gone to one in Mattapan. He remembered because they had tried to guess what the letters in the name stood for:

INTERESTING GREEN APPLES
INTERNATIONAL GRAPES AVAILABLE
ISLAND GROCERIES ALWAYS

IRATE GRUMPY ASSOCIATES
INCREDIBLE GRAINS ADVERTISED
IMPERIAL GRAY ASPHALT

Every idea was unbelievably stupid, but they had had fun just the same.

So, he could get off at the IGA, but he suspected it would be in a pretty populated area, and he would need to find a place to camp out. The bus wouldn't arrive until about four; it was dark these days by seven—kind of late to begin walking south. Plus, he was tired from all the trips he'd already taken between Mrs. Olson's farm and Bar Harbor.

The stop before the IGA was a campground called Narrows Too. Jack didn't have money for a campsite, but he figured a campground would be closer to wilderness—wilderness where he could hide for the night. Decision made. He'd get off at Narrows Too.

Unfortunately, the campground wasn't at all what Jack had imagined. It was on the main highway and wide-open—a place intended for RVs rather than small tents. It would be difficult to sneak into and even more difficult to hide in. He decided to walk up and down the road to see what else was in the surrounding area.

The smell of steamed lobster drew him toward the Trenton Bridge Lobster Pound. Outside were six wood-burning vats with steam rising from them. Oh, how he wished he could have a plate of steamed mussels or a lobster right now! He could taste the warm butter and tender meat. Or a roll! Even just a roll!

After pitching the potatoes into the woods on his walk back to Bar Harbor—he'd have had no way to cook them, and he didn't think you could eat them raw—Jack had finished a green pepper and another cereal bar, but these didn't satisfy him after so much walking and carrying. He wished he were a mangy dog right now that could crawl under one of the outdoor picnic tables and beg for scraps.

Maybe he should have kept the potatoes. He probably could have bartered for something. Would they have thought it cute if he'd offered to trade some homegrown potatoes for a lobster roll? It seemed like every decision he made had good consequences (his bag was lighter) and bad (he had nothing to offer anyone else). He'd have to do a better job of thinking things through.

While standing there, taking in the torturous smells, Jack began reading the license plates of the cars parked off to the side. It was an old habit. Since his mom did so much driving, she played the license-plate game over and over again. She'd seen all fifty states three times now. Not many people could claim to have seen a Hawaiian plate three times. Well, OK, if you lived in Hawaii, you could. Jack's favorite was the one from Tennessee—it had an elephant on it.

There wasn't a single Maine plate in this parking lot. There were two cars from Connecticut, a minivan from New Jersey, and a pickup truck from Massachusetts.

Massachusetts? He looked around as if the faces of the people going in and out could reveal their state identity. What if the driver of the pickup was heading south? He could ride with them. He could be home tonight! He imagined the conversation in his head.

"Hey, are you on your way south? Me too! Would you mind giving me a ride?"

He was being stupid. No one was going to willingly transport a kid without his parents' permission. They'd guess he was a runaway. They'd call DSS in a nanosecond. Still, it was an idea that was hard to let go of.

Jack went inside the lobster shack, allowing the screen door to slam behind him. It was a friendly place, with mint-green walls and bright-red benches. Fishing nets cradling colorful glass balls and starfish hung from the ceiling. There was a chips rack right next to the door—what Jack wouldn't do for a bag of salt-and-vinegar chips—and he hung back by the rack to see if he could figure anything out.

In the dining room to his left was a couple, probably in their eighties, Jack guessed, seated at a table, waiting for their order. At the table next to theirs were an Asian mother and daughter, speaking a language Jack couldn't understand.

A woman with curly gray hair was standing at the counter, placing an order, asking if they had a traditional lobster roll. A teenage girl with braces tried to answer politely, but she was clearly confused by what the woman meant.

"Ours is the traditional," said another woman in an apron—probably the owner of the lobster pound. "Everyone ate lobster salad on bread before the hot-dog bun became so popular."

Jack took a deep breath and walked over to the older couple like it was the most natural thing in the world and asked, "Excuse me, are you from Massachusetts?"

"What's that?" asked the older man, squinting at Jack.

"Are you from Massachusetts? I noticed a truck outside with Mass. plates. I'm from Jamaica Plain," Jack said.

"Melrose," the woman said, leaning toward Jack.

"North of Boston," said the man. "About four and a half hours from—"

"These for here?" the girl behind the counter interrupted.

"Come again?" asked the woman.

The girl repeated the question.

This time the woman understood. "Oh. No.

We're going to take them back with us," she said, preparing to leave.

Take them back. They were going home. Home to Massachusetts. He had to think fast. "Have a good trip!" he called, and hurried outside. Vehicles had begun to park directly in front of the lobster pound, but he knew exactly which truck belonged to the older couple. It was the gray Silverado parked on the side. He brushed by a family with young children and went directly to the truck, acting as if it belonged to him, as if he had decided to wait for his parents, or his grandparents, outside.

The truck was fairly high off the ground and had one of those extended cabs with the little seats in the back. Could he hide back there?

Think, Jack. Don't be too quick this time. They'd have lobsters. They'd put them behind their seats. They'd see him when they did. Besides, he could clearly see that the cab was locked.

The bed. He glanced at the other parked vehicles to make sure no one was seated inside and watching him. All were empty. Then he stepped right up on the truck's bumper and took a good look in the back. There were lots of wood chips and a crumpled tarp. Could he hide beneath the tarp? Would they see him then? And what if they did?

What would he do?

He'd run. Certainly, he could outrun this couple. He'd be gone and hiding before the police arrived.

Before anyone else pulled into the lot, Jack jumped into the back of the truck, scurried under the tarp, and lay there facedown. He could flatten himself fairly well but realized his backpack must be bulging. He slowly and quietly pulled his backpack off and tucked it under him, hoping to compress it as best he could. He thought of pulling his sleeping bag out, but that would make running away, if he had to, harder.

Jack's heart was beating so loudly, he was thankful the couple was hard of hearing. Certainly, anyone else could hear the *bang, bang, bang* coming from his chest, or his breathing, which sounded as if he'd just run a marathon.

Voices. There was some good-natured shouting and laughing; he was pretty sure it was the

Massachusetts couple. He heard the cab open, the front seat snap as it lurched forward (presumably so they could put the lobsters in the back of the cab), and then the engine start up.

He had done it. He hadn't been seen. He didn't know if the couple had glanced in the back of the truck, but he did know that he was undiscovered. He'd be back in his own state in four hours. Of course, he wouldn't be in Jamaica Plain, but he would sure be a whole lot closer.

His stomach rumbled, and he realized then that he'd left his bag of vegetables under the picnic table, but it didn't matter. He'd be home, having a can of ravioli, before the night was over. He hadn't found his mom, but this was the next-best thing.

Jack knew that the truck would travel for some time on smaller, busy roads and that then eventually they'd be on the Maine Turnpike. Speeding along on the highway at sixty-five miles per hour would be cold. At that point, Jack told himself, he could take his sleeping bag out and wrap himself up in it. It wasn't likely they'd hear him then.

So he was surprised when the truck seemed

to be driving on a very bumpy road. *Maybe it just feels bumpier when you're in the back,* he thought. Or maybe they knew a shortcut, which would be cool.

The truck came to a stop.

Were they at a gas station? Were they picking up other supplies or souvenirs before heading back? He listened to both doors opening and shutting. Then he heard the slamming of a screen door— twice. He made himself stay still for a moment or two more. When he was certain the couple was out of sight, Jack slowly lifted his head and peeked out from under the tarp.

All he could see were trees.

He sat up farther.

Ahead of him was a cottage—clearly a summer home. Because the little house was shaded, and because sunset was not far off, lights snapped on. Jack could see the couple moving around in the kitchen, preparing to eat their lobsters.

No!

It couldn't be.

He crawled out of the truck and looked around. There was nothing. No streetlights, no shops, no major roads—hardly any neighbors.

"We'll take them back" had not meant "We'll take them back to Massachusetts." It had meant "We'll take them back to our summer place, our place in the boondocks here in Maine."

Jack felt like he might throw up. He crouched to keep his stomach from revolting. He was certainly way off track now. He figured they'd been driving for twenty minutes—that would take at least three hours to walk! He had no idea where he was, no idea how to get back. He doubted there was a library or an Internet connection for miles. He supposed he could just start walking, but he was tired and hungry—and he'd left the vegetables behind!

He sat down and ripped open a cereal bar, trying to think of what to do next. Tears ran down his cheeks. He couldn't help it. He was trying so hard to be smart, to figure things out. He remembered something his mom had said on their way up to Maine: "I can't do everything for you, Jack. I know you didn't get the mother of your dreams. So what? That's why you have to be smarter than most boys. More independent."

They'd been arguing. She had gotten increasingly agitated. Jack couldn't think about it now. He got up and took a look around. He'd make something up if the couple saw him—how he'd come to borrow a cup of sugar or something.

There were no outbuildings near this cottage. No barn or garage or shack. If he slept here, he'd have to sleep under the stars—just him and his sleeping bag. The ground would be cold. He wished it were the old days and he could just knock on the door and ask if they had a bed he could sleep in.

A bed. That was it. He'd sleep in the truck bed tonight. He'd have to wake early and hide, though. Maybe hide back under the tarp and hope the couple drove back to Trenton, or Ellsworth, or some other town on Jack's route.

A back door to the cottage opened, and Jack froze. He was standing under a tall pine, hoping he was well hidden in the evening shadows.

There was the unmistakable sound of a tin trash-can lid being lifted and then slamming. The remains of the couple's lobster dinner were no doubt in that can. Jack wondered if they'd left any parts in the shell. Imagining the taste of sweet lobster meat got the best of his judgment. As soon as the back door banged shut, Jack made his way to the trash can.

Lifting the lid off without making noise was a slow but rewarding process. He didn't think about how gross it was to be eating someone else's food—food from a trash bin. He flicked a piece of lettuce off half a buttered roll and stuffed it into his mouth. He used his dirty fingernails to break away the stubborn, remaining shell of a lobster claw and popped the leftover meat in his mouth, too. *Slow down,* he told himself. *This is lobster. Taste it.* Then he broke off one of the spindly legs from a lobster's discarded body and sucked the juice from it.

The blaring of a TV inside reminded Jack that the couple could not hear well. Heck, he could probably let himself in and fix himself a meal in the kitchen, and they wouldn't even know it. He stood for a moment at the back door, listening to a news report about a robbery at a grocery store in Bangor—and then to another report. A story about a missing boy. A boy who might be on Mount Desert Island. People were encouraged to get in touch with the police if they knew anything about him.

For a brief moment, relief washed over Jack. They were looking for him! They knew he needed help! He could stop running and turn himself in! But then his head cleared, and a terrible sinking feeling filled his near-empty stomach. Something didn't add up. His mother wouldn't have gone to the police. She'd have known they'd take him from her. Maybe she was so worried about him that she'd risk it. But she'd never worried before. . . .

Who else? The woman from the bookstore? Had she reported the theft? But how would she know he was a missing person and not just some local kid or a tourist? Maybe Big Jack had put things together. Jack didn't think he'd given that much away, though.

They hadn't given any particulars about the boy, had they? It might not be him. He'd read about a missing girl on his first day on the island. Maybe this was something that happened frequently on an island—an island that had a national park.

And even if his mother had initiated the search, would she realize what she'd done? Would she realize how much trouble this would mean for the two of them? (If she was spinning, she might not be thinking straight. She might have gone back to the campground, seen that Jack was gone, and thought someone had kidnapped him. That was what the spinning times where like. She lost all sense of the order of things.)

He'd have to find out more. He'd look online tomorrow. There were lots of ways to figure out who started the search. If the reports didn't mention his finger, it was probably his mother. If they did mention his finger, it was someone else—someone who had put the pieces together.

Jack had to be smart. He had to protect them both. For now, he would continue on his own, continue to lie low.

Thirteen

Elephants, when laughed at, have been known to fill their trunks with water to spray those who mock them.

He'd been having wild dreams when he woke, wild, chasing dreams. The truck bed was cold, and worse, it was raining. Big, heavy drops were beating down on the tarp. Fortunately, Jack had crawled under it last night, preferring to be hidden from sight rather than out in the fresh air.

He slipped on the extra shirt and his Windbreaker and pulled a cereal bar from his backpack. He ate as slowly as he could, hoping it would feel as if he'd had a full meal by the time he finished. Also, by concentrating on every bite, he didn't have to think about what came next. He sort of wished the *What next?* would take care of itself. Like, maybe the couple would come out, throw their suitcases in the back, and say, "OK, we'd better get going if we want to get back to Melrose in time to see the Red Sox game."

Of course, if they lifted up the tarp to cover their suitcases, there would be major problems. It might be better if he figured a few things out for himself. He crawled out from under the tarp and, keeping his head down, jogged toward the cottage. The rain made him brave. He scooted onto the front porch and crouched beside a wicker chair. The chair was under a window, and although the window was closed, the couple spoke loudly enough to be heard.

They were playing Scrabble. First thing in the morning. Like they didn't have a care in the world other than how to get a triple-word score. Jack slid down, sitting on the porch with his back against the wall of the house, and listened. There was no planning, no talk of a schedule, no clues about when they might get into their truck and drive out of here. It definitely didn't look as if they were getting ready to go anywhere.

Way too impatient to sit around on a porch all day, he decided to pack up his things and start walking. Heck, a little bit of rain never hurt anyone.

There seemed to be only one main road, and he could see from time to time that the ocean was on his left. Both of these facts reassured him: he couldn't take a wrong turn, and he had to be heading south. After walking for forty-five minutes in the pelting rain, making sure to turn left at a fork, Jack ducked under the extended roofline of a school. A plaque told him that it was the Lamoine Consolidated School, which probably meant that he was in the town of Lamoine—wherever that was! He was drenched.

"Are you going in, sir?" asked a woman who had rushed up and was now closing her umbrella. She said it in that voice teachers use when you're temporarily out to lunch.

"No—no, I don't go to school here. I was just getting out of the rain."

"Where *do* you go to school, if you don't go here?"

"I go to school in—" He started to say *Massachusetts* but stopped himself. What if she had seen another news story about the missing boy? What if they had said the boy was from Massachusetts? (He'd already told the librarian as much, he remembered.) "I mean, I used to go to school, but now I'm homeschooled."

"Then what are you doing here, soaked like a washrag?"

His left hand folded around the little elephant in his pocket. It gave him comfort. It gave him courage. "I returned some supplies we borrowed," he said, and then, for effect, pointed to his backpack. Wow, he should be a spy or something when he grew up. He was becoming a professional liar.

"Well, you'd better get on home, then. This rain isn't going to stop any time soon." She entered the school.

Jack nodded—though the woman hadn't even waited for a response—and headed back down the road.

He was pleased to have stumbled upon the perfect excuse for being out of school on a Wednesday.

But it didn't exactly come out of nowhere. When he was nine, his mother was asked to attend a meeting at school—a meeting because the school guidance counselor had concerns. After the meeting, she told Jack she was thinking of yanking him out. "You won't be homeschooled, Jack. You'll be unschooled. You'll learn the ways of the world through experience, without all these silly adults, with their silly rules and their silly concerns, breathing down our necks."

That was the same month she had just shown up at school three different times and pulled him out for the day. The last time was during morning announcements.

"I hope nothing's wrong," his teacher had said.

"Doctor's appointment," his mother had replied.

Jack had gathered up his stuff, asked his homeroom teacher (who was also his English teacher) for his homework assignment (knowing he was going to fall further behind), and followed his mother out the door. "But I'm not sick," he had said.

"I know, honey. It's a regular checkup. All kids have regular checkups."

"They do? Why?"

She'd begun talking about vaccinations and how sometimes a little dose of one thing could prevent something worse from happening and how visiting the doctor was like that—you got a little dose of doctoring so that you wouldn't need a bigger dose of hospitalization later—but it was one of those times when he hadn't felt smart enough to follow what she was saying, so he'd just buckled up and hoped it didn't mean he was getting a shot, like the one he had to get when he stepped on a nail at the construction site near Nina's high-rise. Her mother had insisted.

They'd driven for a long time that day, and Jack had begun thinking that maybe he had some rare disease and had to see a special doctor in a special city, or maybe they were moving again. But no, Mom had pulled into the parking lot of Canobie Lake Park, which had (according to the sign) more than eighty-five rides, games, and attractions.

"Which is going to keep you healthier?" she'd asked. "Someone poking at you with God knows what or a ride on the Corkscrew Coaster?"

Jack still didn't know if he'd had a doctor's appointment that day or not. But he did know that the Corkscrew Coaster was undoubtedly the coolest ride he'd ever been on.

After another twenty minutes of trudging through the rain, he arrived at the Lamoine General Store. Not only was his backpack soaked, but so was his sleeping bag inside. It was getting heavier by the minute.

Confident in his new lie about homeschooling, he went inside to dry out. It didn't occur to him that the store would be so little (only three open aisles, with a lunch counter in the front) and he would be so obvious. He slipped into one of the aisles and pretended to be studying the wide assortment of snack food. Every now and then, he glanced toward the front of the store. Two women in hairnets were working behind the counter. One was making cheesesteak sandwiches on the grill; the other was at the register, cashing out a man who was wearing a T-shirt that read, *The way life should be.* Two men sat at the counter, waiting for their lunch.

"What is it you're looking for, kid?" asked one of the guys at the counter. The man was about forty,

Jack guessed, dressed in grungy, paint-splattered clothes. Even though both his face and his voice were ragged, his eyes were smiling.

"Just looking," said Jack. He involuntarily shivered as he said this.

"Shouldn't you be in school?" asked the second guy—a younger guy, maybe the first one's son—whose clothes were also covered in paint but whose eyes were definitely less kind.

"Homeschooled," Jack said, trying to muster up some authority in his voice.

The young one snickered and whispered, "Mama's boy."

Jack's face prickled. *Yeah, I'm some mama's boy. That's why I'm stranded in Maine, standing here soaked to the bone. I haven't eaten a full meal in days. I've slept on the ground, in a barn, and in a truck.*

"So, does being homeschooled make you smarter than the average Lamoine kid?" asked the older guy.

"Ralph," said one of the women as she flipped the sandwiches onto plates.

"I'm not from Lamoine," Jack blurted before he could catch himself.

"You don't say," said the younger guy, laughing.

"Hey," said Ralph, reaching for a newspaper next to him on the counter, "are you that kid—?"

Jack didn't wait to hear what he was going to say. He bolted out of the Lamoine General Store and ran as fast as a kid drenched from head to toe and carrying a heavy backpack could run.

Dang it! Now what was he going to do? He imagined the guys in the store being just interested enough that they'd call the police, tell them they'd seen the kid. Not only would the police know exactly where he was; they'd search harder. How was he going to walk south with the police looking for him?

For the next hour, there were woods on both sides of the road. Jack walked as close to the tree line as he could, ducking into the trees whenever a car approached. Because of the rain, cars had their headlights on, so he could see them approaching— hopefully before they caught sight of him.

At one point he passed a sand pit with rusty metal sculptures lining the road. There were Jesus fish, flat angels with thin lips and triangle noses;

cutouts of men and women holding hands, of Jesus touching the finger of a man; and signs that said LOVE, PEACE, and JUSTICE in giant letters. But there were also several hand-painted signs with runny letters that reminded Jack of blood, signs that read: NO TRESPASSING: VIOLATORS WILL BE PROSECUTED. He ran on that stretch of road until all the sculptures and all the words felt far behind him.

Finally, this road merged with a busier road, one with fewer trees and more businesses. There were auto-parts stores, paint stores, and shoe stores. Maybe, Jack thought, it was better to be in a crowded place. He wouldn't call attention to himself.

By this time, his bare legs felt so cold from the constant rain, he could hardly feel them. Except, that is, for the places where his shorts were rubbing against them, making them red and irritated. He'd choose another place to go in and dry off. Someplace that would have lots of people, so that maybe he wouldn't be noticed. Someplace that didn't sell newspapers.

Up ahead was a building that looked more like a camp lodge than a store. The sign below the green metal roof read L.L. BEAN OUTLET. Framing the door were kayaks that reminded Jack of Life Savers candies, especially the orange-and-yellow-striped ones. "No one goes to Maine without shopping at L.L. Bean," his mother had said when they were making their list.

Why would everyone want to go to an outdoor-sports store? he had wondered. Now here he was—only this one didn't look like the store in the picture his mom had shown him. There was no giant boot out front, either. This must be a baby L.L. Bean.

At the front of the store was a rack of bikes, and some sports accessories like compasses and water bottles, but the rest of the store was a field of clothes—clothes, and tourists carrying canvas shopping bags instead of pushing carts. It wasn't until Jack had woven his way through the mob (keeping his head down and apologizing over and over for his bulky backpack) that he saw a smattering of camp furniture in the corner. He imagined himself stretching out on the futon and taking a nap. *Yeah, right.* How long would it take for someone to recognize him as the kid on the news?

Jack had learned his lesson. He needed to rest and

dry off, but he'd have to remain hidden this time. It didn't take long to come up with a perfect plan.

He went to a rack of boys' clothes and grabbed a striped shirt and an L.L. Bean sweatshirt. He hunted for shorts or pants, but they didn't seem to have any of those today—at least not any where he was standing—so he grabbed a bathing suit instead. Then he went into one of the men's dressing rooms, where the walls, benches, and doors were pinewood. It was the last dressing room before the handicapped one. He locked the door and slipped out of his wet clothes and into the ones he'd gathered. The shirt was huge, but it didn't matter. He wasn't going to take these clothes; he was just going to borrow them for a while. After setting the elephant on the bench, he hung his own clothes up on the metal hooks to dry. Finally, he stretched out on the wooden bench and pulled out his comic books, but the pages were stuck together and ripped at the slightest touch. Practically pulp.

He pulled the big shirt over his still-cold legs. He ate a cereal bar. These bars that the man at the food pantry had picked out were filling, but boy, was he getting sick of this one nutty, raisiny flavor.

Every now and again, someone would knock and he'd say, "I'm in here," and then they'd pop into another stall. For a long time, he just sat there, listening to the sounds of the voices nearby. Mostly, they were the voices of women telling their husband or their son if something looked right. He smiled as he thought of what his own mother would say about his new outfit. Didn't matter. He was finally warm.

He kept thinking: *You should go now. It's time to put on your own clothes and slip out of here,* but he couldn't force himself to move.

He picked up his elephant and studied her again. She had these cute folds of skin on her breastbone — skin she was meant to grow into, he guessed. He thought he should name her. First, he thought of the obvious names: Ellie, Ella, Dumbo (whoever came up with that name didn't really know elephants), Horton, Lydia (like the one here in Maine, the one who had started everything with him and his mom).

No, he wouldn't name her Lydia. He tried to think of other elephant names from real life, from circuses or elephant sanctuaries. He'd only seen one elephant, and he didn't remember her name. Maybe he'd never known it. Twice, his class had taken a field trip to the zoo, but neither the Stone Zoo nor the Franklin Park Zoo had elephants. For years, he'd begged and begged his mother to take him to the circus whenever it came to Boston, but the one time she bought tickets, she forgot and didn't come home that night. After that, she began talking about how cruel circuses were to elephants and how she wasn't going to support them, and how could he, a kid who loved elephants, even think of supporting that sort of thing?

He couldn't explain it. He could never explain to other kids why elephants mattered so much to him; nor could he explain to his mother how much he just wanted to see one again—to reach out and feel its skin, touch its trunk, look into its big, lonely elephant eyes.

Lots of sites on the Internet—like the ones for elephant orphanages—had live cams of elephants or provided videos. He'd watched two elephants who hadn't seen each other for years go nuts after meeting again. He'd seen a video of an elephant whose best friend was a stray dog. ("Like you and me," Nina had said, laughing.) And he'd heard an elephant keeper say that if you blow softly into the trunk of an elephant, it will never forget you.

This was the last thought he had before dozing.

He woke to shouting. Not frantic or angry shouting, but the kind of yelling people do when they're talking across a distance. It took him a moment to remember where he was, but it didn't take him long to realize that the shouting was coming from the people who worked at the store and that they were calling out to one another. Closing time.

Dang! Should he change? Maybe he should just grab his own clothes and run — take off before they had a chance to wonder why a kid was hanging out in a dressing room by himself. Or maybe . . .

He gathered his damp clothes in his arms and quietly opened the door, just a crack — just far enough that the stall would appear unoccupied. Then he huddled on the bench in the corner that was blocked by the door.

He could hear footsteps nearby and held his breath: a girl humming, the opening of another dressing-room door.

After what seemed like an eternity, he heard her shout, "All clear!"

The lights went out.

Jack was going to spend the night in the store.

Fourteen

Ruby, an elephant in Phoenix, Arizona, paints. Jealous of the attention she gets, the other elephants began using the ends of logs to make drawings on the walls.

Eventually, Jack's eyes adjusted to the dark; still, he reached into his backpack and pulled out his flashlight. Would it work? He knew that wet batteries corroded, but it hadn't been wet that long. His thumb pushed on the switch—

Light!

As he moved out of the dressing room and into the main part of the store, he realized how foolish he was being. People outside could probably see the flashlight beam through the large windows. They would think the store was being robbed!

Flashlight off!

The store was even cooler when it was empty. There was the futon to stretch out on, and plenty of warm, dry sleeping bags to borrow for the night hanging on the back wall.

The first thing Jack did was head to the main doors to make sure he'd be able to let himself out come morning. To his relief, he noted that just above the handle was one of those half-circle locks you simply have to turn and a bolt moves side to side. Now he just had to hope opening the doors from the inside wouldn't trigger an alarm. But he'd deal with that tomorrow.

Next he explored the camping accessories on the shelf near the front of the store. He found a box labeled *First-Aid Kit for Sporting Dogs* and wondered if it would have dry gauze for his cold and achy finger. Sure enough, it was on the list of enclosed items, but something prevented Jack from just tearing into the package. Except for when he took the elephant, Jack had never deliberately stolen from a store. He decided he'd rewrap his finger using the old gauze once it had dried out.

But what about food? He only had one cereal

bar left. Wasn't taking food—something you absolutely needed—different from taking something just because you could? He was pretty sure that if the owner of L.L. Bean knew about his situation, he'd want him to eat.

Jack looked around to see if there was anything edible. Maybe they would have that freeze-dried stuff hikers ate. Once, Nina had gotten a bag of freeze-dried beef stew from her uncle for Christmas. They'd mixed it up together, and at the time, it had tasted pretty awful, but he bet he'd like it now.

Unfortunately, the only food items he could find in the store were maple syrup, different flavored jams, and gummy worms in a fake tackle box. All of it sounded really unappealing (what he wouldn't give for a Big Mac), but he broke into and ate a package of gummy worms anyway. For some reason, they tasted worse than he expected.

He grabbed his water bottle and filled it up in the single restroom. When he came out, he noticed two large swinging doors with small windows at the top. He stood on his tiptoes and peered into a large room filled with boxes of inventory. There seemed to be as much merchandise in the back room as there was in the store. He started to back away from the doors, knowing they were for employees only, and then realized it didn't matter. Tonight he could go anywhere he wanted to—he could see it all. He pushed cautiously on the right-hand door; he was entering a forbidden world.

Shelves were lined with boxes of sunglasses, fishing rods, and wading boots. *It must be fun to work here,* he thought, especially if you got to be the one to open the boxes, to see what you'd be selling that week. But the storage room wasn't the only section off-limits to customers. On the far side of the room was another door. It also had a window, but a curtain blocked the view of what was inside. This time he didn't hesitate. He went over and turned the knob.

It was a small room with a large table, a couch, and a tiny kitchen area, but to Jack it looked luxurious. He went directly to the refrigerator and found leftover lunches: partially eaten sandwiches, mysterious Tupperware containers, an apple, a can of Diet Coke. In the freezer were Lean Cuisine meals. He looked around and spotted a microwave. He was going to have a feast!

Right after he finished investigating.

Off the little room were two doors. Jack tried the first, but it was locked. He tried the second and thought it might be locked also, but it was simply stuck. With a little extra push, the door swung open to reveal a small office—an office with a computer, a computer that was no doubt hooked up to the Internet.

For the first time in days, Jack did a happy dance, whooping and hollering and jumping in place. He wasn't sure what to do first—go make dinner or check the Internet for reports about the missing boy and his mom. He made himself calm down. *You have all night,* he told himself.

So he ate. He ate half a turkey sub and the apple. Then he zapped some lasagna and a frozen panini. He felt like he should keep eating, but his stomach must have shrunk over the past five days. One more bite and he would barf for sure. He stretched out on the couch for a while to give his stomach a break. And that's when he saw it: a small TV hanging from the wall above him. He located the remote control between two cushions on the couch and turned it on. For a few moments, he was content to watch reruns of *The Simpsons,* and then he realized the news was probably on. Maybe he'd catch the story about the missing boy. He switched channels, but stories about fighting in countries he'd hardly heard of made him impatient. Jack turned off the TV and went into the office to use the computer instead.

Fortunately, the computer was not password protected. In no time at all, he was checking both his YouPage (*No messages from Nina—weird*) and his mom's. Still no cyber signs of her. So he held his breath and searched for *missing boy maine.* He was dying to know if the reports were about him and, if so, who had gone to the police.

His picture came up immediately on a Bangor news website. Not only was it his picture staring back at him, but it had the word *Play* written across his chest. He clicked on it to watch a video of the actual broadcast.

He watched it three times in a freaky kind of amazement. His grandmother (his *grandmother?*) had gotten a call from a man en route to the Bahamas, and although she couldn't understand much from the call, she'd figured out that his mother was headed there and he was not. So she called the only other person she could think of: Nina. Nina had told Gram that he and his mother had been vacationing in Maine and that Jack hadn't returned for school. Nina. The only person on this planet other than his mom who knew him from the inside out. Who knew that the last thing he'd want was for anyone, *especially* his grandmother, to know where he was and what had happened.

His grandmother had called the Maine State Police, who reported having found a tent and an air mattress in the woods. After the news story aired yesterday, Mrs. Olson reported seeing Jack at her farm. The food-pantry guy, the woman from Sherman's (who mentioned his broken finger to the reporter), the Island Explorer bus driver, and one of the women from the Lamoine General Store had also come forward.

He got up and paced around the small room.

Concentrate! he told himself. Just because people were looking for him did not mean he would be found. He just had to think.

He took his wet sleeping bag out of his backpack and placed it over the table to dry. He retrieved his still-damp clothes from the dressing room and hung them off the chairs. He looked in the refrigerator for any food that he could carry with him. He selected some packaged veggies and dip, a slice of pepperoni pizza, and a questionable-looking piece of birthday cake, and packed them in the outside pockets of his backpack. It was like the time they predicted a really big blizzard in Boston. He and his mom went into preparation mode, buying canned goods and water, getting out the candles. He knew he was preparing now; he just didn't know for what.

Streetlights lit up the store well enough for Jack to see without the flashlight. He grabbed one of the dry L.L. Bean sleeping bags and began to curl up on the couch in the staff room. That's when he noticed it: BO—his own! Even though he'd been out in the rain all day, he was really beginning to stink. Maybe it was time to take a sponge bath.

About twenty scratchy, soapy paper towels later, he crawled into the sleeping bag and turned the TV on, but he didn't hear a word that was spoken. His mind went in circles.

He knew that the moment he came out of

hiding or was found, his life would change forever. He would no longer live with his mother. He would no longer live two bus stops away from Nina, and maybe no longer even go to Curley Middle School. He thought of Nina—Nina, who should have known that even hinting that his mother wasn't taking good care of him, hinting to his *grandmother,* of all people, could ruin everything.

His thoughts turned to his grandmother. She had looked older—older and worried. But the worried part, that was probably just for show. His mother had told him that ever since she was a little girl, her mother had tried to control her, tried to destroy her life. "She's crazy, Jack," his mother had said. "You have to trust me on this." Now, once again, his grandmother was trying to take him away from his mother. And this time she'd probably succeed.

It would serve Mom right, Jack thought, but immediately regretted it.

He reached for his still-unnamed elephant. His mom was spinning, and she couldn't be held responsible for what she did during the spinning times. Maybe he could find a way to get to the Bahamas, too. Maybe they could live there, where people wouldn't know anything about them and wouldn't even consider taking him away from her. They could live in a hut on the beach. Catch fish. Maybe after thinking about what she had done, she'd stay on her medication forever. (She had promised that before. Still . . .)

He thought of getting back on the computer and blasting Nina but had heard that people could be traced by their computer activity. Now that he knew they were looking for him, he wouldn't be signing on to his YouPage again.

Fifteen

During World War II, authorities in Tokyo worried that the zoo would be bombed and the escaped animals would be dangerous. By order, all animals were to be poisoned, but the elephants refused to eat their poisoned food.

He had to have more time to figure things out. How could he travel without being seen? Maybe in the dark. He could travel at night now and not during the day. But the thought of walking the dark roads at night, by himself, made him shiver.

If only there was a subway in Maine, or a bus system like the Island Explorer for the rest of the state. He didn't have money, but he could have stowed away.

There had to be a faster way to travel.

Wait a minute . . . what about a bike? There were all those bikes in the front of the store. No one would expect a missing kid to be riding a bike somewhere. Especially if he was wearing a helmet! And his identity would be well hidden beneath a helmet. He wouldn't have to travel at night after all.

He went back out front and inspected the bikes by flashlight. There were six bikes there—two about the right size for him—and none of them were locked. Boy, things sure were different in Maine.

Light suddenly flashed into the store.

Jack ducked behind the bikes and turned his flashlight off. A car had pulled into the parking lot, and its headlights had swung into the store.

His heart threatened to leap right out of his chest.

Had someone seen him? Seen his flashlight beam and called the police? Did they think he was robbing the store?

A man got out of the car and tried the door. The rattle echoed in the building. Was it a cop? The glaring headlights made it hard to tell.

Jack held his breath; still, the flashlight shook in his left hand. At any moment he expected a voice from a bullhorn to tell him to stay where he was.

The sound of a radio—a walkie-talkie radio— came from the car. It had to be the police, didn't it? The officer went back to the car, slammed the car door behind him. Jack lifted up his head and watched the now-visible cruiser move on.

He let out a gust of air and sat there, his head resting on his knees, until he could no longer feel his blood banging against the walls of his veins.

A dog barked in the distance.

And I was worried about eating the gummy worms, he thought. *If I get caught stealing a bike, I'm going to juvie.*

Was it worth it? Was stealing a bike worth the risk?

One of the things his mom always said when teachers and guidance counselors started poking into their business was, "Can't they see what a good kid you are? Can't they see that I'm raising you right?"

Would stealing a bike mean that Jack had proved the opposite? Maybe he was turning out to be a bad kid after all.

But what were his choices? Without the bike, he would have to walk at night. Wouldn't that be more dangerous? He could explain, he reasoned, that with the bike, he was being smart, playing it safe — doing what his mother had taught him.

He pulled himself up and went back to the computer to figure out logistics. He hadn't biked in a long time — not since the time he and his mother rented bikes and rode around Jamaica Pond. And that was a really easy ride. He pulled up a map of the area. He could take the Maine Turnpike home, but he remembered seeing a sign: no bikes, horses, or walkers allowed. Plus, he'd probably be more noticeable riding along a major highway. So he investigated the minor routes and finally decided on Route 1. He'd try to get to Bucksport — which was about twenty miles away — tomorrow. Jack printed the map.

He knew he was being ambitious; he'd have to leave pretty early if he planned to make it that far. Would the employees notice a bike was missing, or would they think it had been sold? He realized that right now, anyone could tell that there'd been an intruder. An intruder who had used the microwave. He got up and straightened up as much as he could. He threw the frozen-food packages and the empty Tupperware containers into the bathroom trash. He grabbed the empty gummy-worm box and did the same with that. He changed into his own clothes and placed the borrowed ones back on the rack. With any luck, the only thing they would notice was the missing food—and hopefully not until lunchtime.

A helmet. He needed a helmet. He hadn't seen any out front, but maybe they had some in the storeroom. He was just about to give up when he noticed a couple of used helmets—one for kids and one for adults—on a shelf near the door. They probably offered the use of those helmets for test rides of the bikes. He tried on the smaller of the two helmets. It would work.

Jack set the computer alarm and left the office door open. Then he curled up on the office couch. He would begin riding at 6:00 a.m.

Sixteen

Elephants' ears are designed to act as an air-conditioning system. As blood passes through an elephant's thin ears, it's cooled by the air and then moves on to cool the whole elephant down. Flapping the ears helps the process.

Riding the bike was scary at first. He had to go through the center of town and didn't know the rules. Should he be riding on the sidewalk or in the street? And what were the laws for intersections? Was he supposed to continue riding, or was he supposed to get off the bike and walk it across? Did he need to wait for the light to turn green, or could he just cross if there were no vehicles coming? At this hour there were hardly any cars, but still, the last thing he needed, now that he was not only running from the police but had stolen a bike, was to be noticed.

He decided to walk across a major intersection. Surely, no one could fault him for being extra cautious. When he got to the other side, he faced his next challenge: Main Street, a road he couldn't avoid, was one long, steep hill—one he had to go down.

He could picture himself losing control of the bike and crashing into one of the cars parked along the side of the street. Or, worse, hitting an oncoming car head-on. He decided to use the sidewalk—and his brakes. Almost immediately, he started speeding down the hill. He panicked and braked hard, nearly catapulting over the top of the handlebars. He started again and braked more gently, easing himself down the hill.

Below him was a bridge. *Great,* he thought, *I'll get to the bottom of the hill, only to bash into a guardrail and go toppling into a river.* But he didn't. With only a little wiggling as he rode next to the railing, he crossed to the other side.

He was through Ellsworth and on his way.

Jack could tell from the map that there would be long parts on the ride with no interesting towns or sights to see, but he couldn't believe how quickly the city turned into country and how amazingly boring the country road to Bucksport was. "Woods and fields and trailers, woods and fields and trailers, woods and fields and trailers," he recited, letting the sound of his own voice be entertainment.

Jack might have dreaded that first big hill in Ellsworth, but it got to the point that he was praying for hills now just to break up the ride. Slopes gave him the chance to coast for a while, and he was gaining the confidence to fly down them. And little by little, he began to figure out the gears on the bike. At first, he was using far more energy on inclines than he needed to. Later, he realized that if he downshifted while coasting, he would gain more traction at the end and would therefore not have to work quite so hard on the next climb.

Not used to biking, his legs felt tight after a couple of hours of riding. He decided to take a break and slip into the bathroom at the gas station up ahead, on the corner of an intersection. He could rest his legs and fill up his water bottle. He parked his bike next to two Dumpsters and left the helmet on the handlebars. He thought of leaving the helmet on his head, since it made him feel more hidden, but (a) he'd feel dorky, and (b) it might give people an invitation to ask him questions about his bike ride.

A woman was purchasing a gallon of milk at the counter, which gave Jack the opportunity to slip into the restroom unnoticed. When he came out, a sunburned man was waiting by the door. The man looked down — down at Jack's wrapped finger (why had he bothered to rewrap it?) — and then up at his face.

"Excuse me," said Jack, moving past the man fast enough to avoid questions, slowly enough to avoid suspicion. He heard the restroom door close behind him and hoped that that was the end of the man's curiosity.

Jack had wanted to take out his map before hopping on his bike, check out his location and the distance he'd traveled, but he didn't dare pause. What he did know was that he was inland now, and the day was beginning to get really hot. He went from wearing his long-sleeved shirt and jacket to just the long-sleeved shirt to his short-sleeved one instead. On one hill, he peeled off his shirt altogether. By the time he reached the Orland River, he knew he was going in. Only problem was, the Orland River was right on the edge of town. Could he take a swim on a Thursday, in the middle of the day, without anyone noticing him? He'd have to stay out of sight of drivers, walkers, and anyone who happened to look out a nearby window at the river below.

He parked his bike in the woods near a bridge, then slid down the embankment and into the water. Although it felt a little creepy under the bridge, he remained there in the semidarkness, where he wouldn't be seen. He swam from one side of the bridge to the other, hoping there weren't snakes or leeches in this river, and boy, did it feel good.

After the swim, he lay down on a sun-baked rock in the woods to dry off. Then he ate the food he'd packed. All of it. He did think it might have been smarter to save some of the food for later, but so far, he'd been able to get food pretty much whenever he needed it, and right now, he was starving. He could always find some more bottles, raid another garden, or hide out in another store. Heck, maybe he'd choose a grocery store tonight!

He didn't feel much like riding after his break,

but he knew he'd better keep going. People might have guessed he'd spent the night in L.L. Bean by now. He needed to get as far away as possible.

Finally, he reached the town of Bucksport. His skin was beginning to feel stretched tight over his face and shoulders, and he suspected a sunburn. Putting on his shirt made his shoulders hurt, confirming his suspicion. Jack was so tempted to stop here, to visit the library, which was surely air-conditioned. But it was simply too risky. He didn't dare use his homeschool excuse—not now, when people were on the lookout for him.

As Jack crossed a bridge in town, he saw a large castle-like structure in the distance. He stopped and pulled out his map: *Fort Knox,* the map said. Ha! He'd heard of Fort Knox. That was where all the gold was kept. But he was pretty sure that that Fort Knox was in the South.

This one looked awesome, and like the perfect place to escape from the sun for a few hours—the sun, and the darn deerflies that buzzed around his head every time he came to a stop. That is, if he could get inside, he thought as he batted the pests away.

After crossing the bridge, he came to another,

one that was perhaps the tallest, coolest bridge he'd ever seen. It was sparkling new, with gleaming silver cables that went up to two towers, one of which, Jack could tell by the windows at the top, was an observation tower. The old bridge still spanned the wide river, just below and to the right of the newer one. Glancing down at the narrow double lanes and the barely waist-high, rusty guardrail on the old bridge, Jack was awfully glad for the renovation. Still, the sheer height of the new bridge made his heart race as he crossed.

Unfortunately, as he pedaled closer, he could see that in the middle of the road, there was a booth at the fort entrance, with several cars in line, waiting to pass through. He glanced up at the sign towering beside him: it was a state park; admission was required. For a moment, he thought of giving up and going back to Bucksport to find a place out of the heat, but the fort had looked so amazing from a distance, and he figured he'd be much safer there, since most vistors would be tourists — people who were less likely to be watching the local news.

There wasn't a fence around the park, he noticed as he looked around. And there seemed to be only one person manning the small booth. Perhaps you only had to pay if you needed parking. Maybe walkers and bicyclists could go right in.

As much as he wanted to believe that might be true, Jack knew it wasn't likely. He knew if he walked his bike up to the booth, he'd be asked to pay, but he *couldn't:* even if he had had the money, he couldn't have risked being recognized. He would have to sneak in.

Jack left his bike and his backpack leaning against a tree along the side of the park, grabbed his water bottle (boy, he couldn't get enough water today), and zigzagged across the lawn, trying to stay as inconspicuous as possible. He reached the back of the fort and then, keeping close to the cement wall, slipped around to the front entrance.

A rush of cool air welcomed him as he ducked inside. It was dimmer inside, too, but he could make out cannon-gun ports, large open chambers, spiral staircases, and long, dark hallways. Too bad he didn't have his flashlight. He would have loved to explore all the nooks and crannies of this place.

Jack wandered the halls, taking it all in. For

the first time since he'd left the campground, he actually forgot that he was hungry. That he had a broken finger and a sunburn. That his mother was missing and that he'd been left in a campground two states away from home. For a while, he was nothing more than a soldier protecting the valuable Maine coast. He raced up one corridor and down the next. He positioned himself behind real cannons and pretended to fire away. It was nice to be the only kid here; he didn't have to feel like he was too old to play games like this. But oh, how he wished Nina were here to see it!

Then he remembered what Nina had done and took it back.

The lower rooms in the fort were even darker and cooler, and water dripped down some of the walls. Although they were initially dark and creepy, it was in these dank cellar rooms that his burned back felt most comfortable.

At one point, he dragged his hand against an outer wall to keep from getting lost in the darkness. The granite felt at times smooth and dry, at other times rough and damp. Jack was picturing worms and mold coating these walls, when *wham!* he bumped right into another, much larger person in the dark.

The man laughed a deep, howling laugh. Jack's heart skipped a beat, and he took off running.

"Hey, kid!" the man yelled. "Come back! I didn't mean to scare you."

But Jack didn't stop, which might or might not have been a good decision. Speaking to strangers could get him recognized; not speaking could raise their concern — or at least their curiosity.

Once around a couple of bends, Jack slowed down. He continued exploring but was careful to watch where he was going. Eventually, he heard the voices of other kids and knew that school must be out. Sure enough, he passed a troop of Cub Scouts, screeching as they entered a dark powder room at the base of the fort. Since these were locals and more apt to know about him, he figured it was time to get his stuff and be off.

Exiting the same way he'd come in, Jack raced toward the clump of trees where he'd hidden his bike. But it wasn't there — nor was his backpack. Was he in the wrong place? He searched in different directions, looking around the entrance from increasing distances. He kept coming back to the same place, where he was fairly certain he'd left his things. It wasn't until he noticed the empty veggie-and-dip wrapper, the one he'd stowed after eating by the river, that he knew that he *was* in the right place. He was in the right place, and everything he'd carried—his extra shirt, his jacket, his flashlight, his sleeping bag—was now gone. Along with the bike.

All Jack had left was a water bottle, the clothes on his back, and one small, plastic elephant.

Seventeen

The Indian elephant is said sometimes to weep.
— CHARLES DARWIN

Jack curled up on a clump of pine needles outside the fort and cried. Not softly, not with the silent tears that had rolled down his face when his mother had said they would not see Lydia. Nor with the frustrated tears that came when he'd ruined his cell phone. No, this cry came from deep in his gut and heaved out of him, causing his chest to hammer against the earth. He moaned between sobs, not caring who heard him now, and let the snot pour down his face.

He was worn out, sunburned, hungry, and lonely, and everything he needed, everything he had counted on, had been stolen.

When the sobs subsided, he remained curled on the ground, hiccuping. He wondered briefly if his things had been taken by people who were searching for him, but that didn't make sense. If they were searching for him, they would have gone into the fort and found him. It wouldn't have been hard. No, it seemed his stuff had been stolen by someone who just wanted the stuff. He'd stolen the bike, and now someone had stolen it from him.

He was tired of thinking of the next step and the next. He wanted this whole trip to end—for it to be one long, bad dream. He wanted to wake up in his own bed and have his mother shout from the kitchen, "Do you want strawberry French toast or an everything omelet for breakfast?"

He wanted someone else to be in charge.

And then, lying there in that pine-needle patch, staring up at the boughs above him, he suddenly didn't want anything at all.

Nothing.

He didn't want to get up. He didn't want to eat.

He didn't want a ride back to Massachusetts. He didn't want to see Nina, or Gram—ever. Didn't want to see his old apartment. He didn't even want a free boat ride to the Bahamas.

Or to ever see his mother again.

Tears rolled down his cheeks once more.

Jack would have stayed there, stayed right there, until some unsuspecting person tripped over him, if it weren't for the setting sun and the onslaught of mosquitoes. He tried to ignore them, like he was trying to ignore the rest of his troubles, but their needle-like mouths pierced his cheeks, his neck, his exposed arms and legs. Their insistent squeal and the increasing stiffness he was feeling from his sunburn forced him to get up and get walking.

He didn't have a plan. Didn't know where he was going or what he was going to do when he got there. He was just heading south, out of habit now more than anything else.

He missed his long-sleeved shirt, not because it was cold, although it was getting cooler, but because it would have given the mosquitoes one less place to suck. He wondered why the bugs, which had been nearly nonexistent on Mount Desert Island, were such a nuisance now.

It was kind of a relief not to be carrying the heavy backpack, but without a bike and helmet, he was fairly conspicuous; anyone passing would wonder whether he was the missing boy. But he no longer cared.

He saw headlights approaching, and he kept his head up, staring right at them. *You too can be on the news tomorrow night. You can be the heroes that find me.*

The Volkswagen Beetle whizzed by. Seemed they didn't care, either.

Neither did the man on the motorcycle.

Jack didn't know why he had bothered trying to go home in the first place. It had been a stupid plan. Even if he could walk like this all the way to Jamaica Plain, even if he could get back to his apartment, how was he going to pay for things? Not just food, but the rent and the electricity bill?

You could get a job, said the ever-hopeful voice in his head.

Sure, he could get a job. Maybe they'd let him wash dishes or something at Ten Tables. Or he could work for Mrs. Harris, downstairs. She always had jobs for him to do.

Sometimes he would tell his mother all he had done for Mrs. Harris in a single afternoon.

"And she only paid you five dollars? Child-labor laws exist for a reason," his mother had said one time. "I think I may need to remind her."

Five dollars was not going to pay the rent.

And what would he do when he wasn't working? He couldn't go to school. No doubt, everyone at Curley Middle School had already heard about his summer vacation. The moment he showed up there, someone was bound to call DSS.

But she could come back.

Shut up.

Headlights were approaching.

She could.

Shut up!

The headlights came closer.

Jack jumped up and down, waving his hands over his head.

The headlights glared.

"Stop!" he yelled.

But the tanker went right on by.

Eighteen

Some seeds do not germinate unless they have passed through an elephant's digestive system.

It was music that made him slow down. There was a church—the Safe Harbor Church, according to the sign—up on the hill to his right, and there was singing coming from inside. Jack had to think a moment. It wasn't Sunday, was it? And besides, services were held in the morning, not at night. Even a nonchurchgoer like him knew that much. So why the singing on a—on a Thursday night? It could be a performance, but the singing started and stopped, started and stopped. Each time it stopped, someone shouted.

It wasn't a performance, he realized. It was a rehearsal. These singers were practicing.

The windows were brightly lit, and he was cold. It was hard to believe that just an hour ago, he was being cooked alive. The moment the sun went down, the heat shut off. He might not have known his future, but at least he knew what he was going to do next.

He waited until the singing resumed; then he opened the large church door and crept inside. Having been to a couple of weddings, both times as his mother's date, he knew what to expect. He knew there would be a big entryway before the main part of the church. And there would be stairs if he was lucky—and he was. Jack tiptoed up the stairs to a small balcony, which mostly housed the organ pipes, but there were also a few rows of seats.

Jack didn't need a seat. He crawled to the front of the balcony, which was surprisingly warm, and stretched out on the floor. Song rose up, and, even though he was too tired to concentrate on the words, it tucked in around him like a soft blanket. He pulled his elephant out and held her above his eyes.

What would his mother say about this elephant?

He could no longer predict her reactions (though she'd be furious if she learned he stole it). When he was little, she used to bring him something elephant almost every week: pictures from the newspaper, elephant Pez, elephant lollipops. Once, she swapped a necklace she was wearing for an elephant key chain owned by a kid in their apartment building. Another time, a guest had told her about a bakery that sold elephant-shaped raspberry tarts, and she drove the Intown Inn van all the way to the North End to buy him one. It had almost gotten her fired. But as he got older, she seemed to get impatient with his obsession—like he should have outgrown it or something.

He wished that elephants were still something they shared. Maybe that was why he'd told her about elephant poo power on the ride up. He'd wanted to remind her one last time about Lydia . . . wanted her to respond like her old self—like the mom who loved to make him happy. He wanted to give her the opportunity to pull off the highway in York and surprise him. But mentioning elephants had only irritated her.

The music climbed right up to the church

rafters and swelled. Jack could distinguish the sound of one female singer with a high voice and one male with a very low voice. All of the other voices seemed to blend into one.

He thought about Lydia, the one and only elephant in Maine. He had discovered her existence on the day he and his mother had left for Mount Desert Island. He and Nina had been goofing around on the Internet and did what he often did: searched for *elephant and* _____ (whatever interested him or came to mind). He'd searched using the terms *elephants and comics, elephants and pie,* and *elephants and toothpaste,* and had learned some pretty crazy things. That morning, he had searched under *elephants and maine* and discovered Lydia.

Lydia was at York's Wild Kingdom. She performed in a show and gave elephant rides to children. Jack had called his mother at work and begged her to put the animal park on the list. (The town of York was on their way!) But she had refused. She used the same old argument: they would be supporting the keeping of elephants in captivity, elephants who were forced to give people rides. His mom wouldn't fund that.

When they had passed the exit and his mom had not turned off, he'd switched from hinting to pleading.

"Mom, I agree with you! But we don't have to fund it. I don't want to pay for a ride; I just want to see a real elephant again!"

His mother had been slowing the car down, going through a toll. "Someday you and I will go to Asia or Africa, Jack. Then you will see an elephant. In Maine, you will see puffins and lobsters — maybe even a moose!"

She'd made him feel like he was four. "So it's OK to *eat* a lobster, but it's not OK to *look* at an elephant?"

"All right, then, we won't eat lobsters, either. We'll do other things on the list."

"I don't care about the stupid list. It's *your* list — not mine. There's not one thing on that list that I want to do."

"You are so stinking selfish, Jack Martel. Do you realize I spend every day of the week driving a hotel shuttle so you can have the things you want—?"

"Like what?"

"Like a computer, a cell phone, vacations. And now that I have a few days off to enjoy myself, you are determined to wreck it."

He should have stopped there; he'd known that. He had felt the small storm brewing in his mother as she'd driven north, known she was becoming increasingly agitated, the way she often did before things went crazy. But he couldn't stop himself.

"*You're* the one who's selfish. You're the one who doesn't take her medication so she'll feel more 'alive.' Who goes off without—"

"Stop it, Jack! Stop it right now!" she'd screamed. She'd pulled over to the side of the road and had ripped up the list. "You've completely ruined this vacation. We'll spend one night in Maine, and then we're heading back home."

They'd hardly talked again that night. Jack had cried silently, then dozed the rest of the way.

The next morning, she was gone.

And now he was starting to wonder if he would ever see her again.

He started to shake. It could have been chills from the sunburn, but he didn't think so. It was as if thinking about the fight was searing the edges of his heart the way he and Nina used to sear the edges of maps to make them look old.

If only he could reverse time and take the whole argument back. If only he had said to himself, *Shut up, Jack. She's not herself—not her true self,* and had stopped. If only he hadn't wanted to see that elephant so badly.

Tears pushed against the backs of his eyeballs, and he reminded himself that it didn't matter. Nothing mattered.

Nothing.

Not anymore.

And then the choir below sang a song he knew: "Morning Has Broken." It was a song his mother sang, usually when she was feeling good: when the spinning had stopped and the sad times had stopped and for a while she would be her new-morning self. She would say, "I'm so, so sorry, Jackie."

And he would say, "It's OK, Mom. Really, look—I'm OK. We're both OK."

"Sweet the rain's new fall." Jack mouthed the words to the song.

And that's when he knew. He knew the *what next*. He knew what he had to do. He couldn't control what happened to him in the long run—whether he'd make it to Jamaica Plain or to the Bahamas . . . whether he'd be scooped up by DSS and handed over to his grandmother, or maybe even placed in foster care. But he did know this. He, Jack Martel, was going to York's Wild Kingdom. He was going to see Lydia.

Not out of anger. It wasn't his way of saying, "I don't care what *you* want, Mom. I'm seeing this elephant."

It was a way of going back to the beginning. To the beginning of the trip, before they had argued. To the beginning, when elephants were something they both treasured. Jack knew that when he finally saw his mother (*Of course I'll see my mother again—of course, I have to*), she'd cry. And he'd be ready. He'd say, "It's OK, Mom. Really. Guess what I did when I was in Maine? I saw the elephant."

And she'd smile and say something like, "Wait till I tell the animal-protection people," but she'd be so glad . . . so relieved to know he'd gone ahead and grabbed a special moment, so happy to know that he was the same old Jack she'd left in Maine. He knew she would.

It would be their new day, their morning broken.

He'd see Lydia. He'd do it for both of them.

He closed his eyes and let the choir sing him to sleep.

Nineteen

Young elephants love to play together. They tussle over sticks, roll upon one another, attack imaginary enemies, and trunk wrestle.

Jack woke as the only person in an otherwise empty church. Despite his sunburn, despite his now-obvious thirst and the lack of a blanket the previous night, he had slept soundly. And he'd dreamed. Dreamed he was riding high on an African elephant. He and the tusked elephant ambled through a lush green forest and then emerged into a field where a large crowd was waiting. In the back of the crowd was a blond woman—smiling, running along, waving her arms. *It's Mom,* Jack had thought while dreaming. *She's come.* And then she'd faded. He closed his eyes and tried to recapture the dream, but it was gone.

Never mind. Today he was headed for York. He stood, stretched, and went down the narrow stairway to find a bathroom—and maybe food. On the opposite side of the church entry was a small office that smelled both musty and of polished wood. There was a desk, a small bookcase with a couple of worn Bibles on one shelf, and two folding chairs. On the corner of the desk was a jam jar holding a few dead marigolds, probably put there last Sunday. In the corner of the little office, Jack found a restroom no bigger than a closet.

One look in the filmy mirror made him realize he was very lucky not to have been seen last night. Anyone could tell from his red, dirt-streaked face that things were not what they should be. He used a bar of soap and some soggy mounds of toilet paper to give himself another sponge bath.

If only finding food was that easy. Jack walked to the back of the church, behind the pulpit, and cautiously opened a door. A modern room had been added on—a meeting area where people probably came for refreshments after church—and it had a little kitchenette. But all the cupboards held were paper goods, serving trays, and stuff for serving coffee: creamer, sugar cubes, stirring sticks. Jack popped a sugar cube into his mouth, pocketed a handful, and checked out the miniature refrigerator. One box of baking soda—that was it. He'd have to find another way to get food.

As Jack was leaving the church, he noticed a lost-and-found box on a bench near the door. Maybe there'd be a jacket inside. No such luck, but he did find a baseball cap that said *Searsport Vikings*. It was a little big, but that was good—it covered more of his face that way. This, he figured, was as good a disguise as anything. He pulled the baseball cap lower and continued walking.

Acorns lined the road, and for a while Jack concentrated on crushing them beneath his feet. He noticed that along this patch of highway, some of the trees' leaves had started to turn red. He remembered the fall when he and his mother had collected leaves and ironed them between wax paper. He'd hung them in his bedroom windows until the wax paper yellowed and began to curl. For some reason, this memory caused his heart to form a fist, but then he reminded himself that he was too old to do that now anyway, and besides, it wasn't like he hadn't had that experience. He had.

And there were things other than leaves to look at on this road. There were a couple of places where flea markets were held; lots of antiques shops, with funky stuff like weather vanes and giant rocking horses out front; even a shop with mini lighthouses all over its lawn. As he popped sugar cubes into his mouth, he kept his eyes peeled for a vegetable garden, but so far, no luck.

Eventually, a sign welcomed him to Searsport, Maine. He wondered why a kid from this town would go to a church that was two hours away but then laughed. A distance that took two hours for him to walk would probably take less than ten minutes to drive. This sure was the slow way to York.

Jack was starving and needed to come up with a plan for finding food. He hadn't noticed a single soda can on his walk that morning. But he wondered if he could risk turning in cans if he did manage to collect some. With his picture all over the evening news, it would be pretty chancy. And there was absolutely no way that he could approach a food pantry. Perhaps if he got off Main Street and headed down one of the side streets in town, he'd spot a garden.

The houses on the side street he chose were fairly close together—no gardens in sight. But he found himself walking behind three kids—kids he guessed to be about his age—on their way to school. They were wearing new jeans, new sneakers, and clean backpacks. It was definitely the first week of school.

Jack imagined Nina sitting in the front row (she always chose a desk in the front, if allowed) in Mr. Giovanni's class at Curley. He wondered if she was still hanging out with the same friends as last year. It used to be just the two of them, until the other kids began to tease them about going steady, and they'd both found other kids to hang with during the day. It was fairly easy, since they were both pretty laid-back. And they never expected to be invited to other kids' homes in the afternoons or on weekends—that's when they hung out with each other. Or used to.

But now that Jack knew he couldn't trust Nina, he doubted he'd ever hang out at her place again.

A brick school loomed ahead, and Jack paused on the sidewalk, wondering if this one, like Curley, had a free-breakfast program. If he simply walked into the cafeteria and grabbed a tray, would anyone question him? Probably. At home, he needed to provide a number—his school number—to get hot lunch.

"Are you new?"

Jack turned and saw a girl standing beside him. She was taller than him, with dark, curly hair and big blue eyes. She was wearing a long white T-shirt, leggings, and black leather boots, and she carried a messenger bag instead of a backpack. Older. She was definitely older than he was.

"N-no," he stumbled. *What's the best answer?* "No. I just remembered I forgot my homework, though." He turned and ran back the way he'd come, hoping she bought it.

If only he *was* new. What he wouldn't give to

be back in school, with regular hours, a regular life. And food.

Back on Main Street, he turned right and found himself heading into the center of town. Rows of old brick buildings lined both sides of the street, which was busy with people bustling to and from their parked cars, many carrying coffee cups. A couple of men, one in a suit and another in a blue uniform, were waiting to use an ATM. Jack pulled his cap even lower as he passed them. He stood across from one group of shops, all connected like Legos, and read the signs: THE GRASSHOPPER SHOP, LEFT BANK BOOKS, COASTAL COFFEE. At the top of the Coastal Coffee sign, Jack read: FREE INTERNET CAFÉ.

What kind of miracle was this? Sure, libraries had computers, but libraries also had librarians who, wanting to be helpful and all, paid close attention to the comings and goings of kids. A coffee shop — now, that was probably different. A coffee shop would be used to tourists — people that no one had ever seen around before. And at this hour of the morning, a café would be busy, with people trying to get to work and to school on time. They'd hardly notice him.

With Internet access, he could get directions to the animal park, plan a route. And, even though he wouldn't allow himself to check his YouPage—not until he'd seen Lydia—there was a small chance that reporters had tracked down his mother, had figured out her whereabouts. Maybe she was back in this country. He'd feel better knowing they were both in the same country again.

Jack climbed the steps of the coffee shop and went inside.

The walls and ceilings were painted periwinkle, Nina's favorite color. Loads of people were seated at tables near the entrance—tables covered in plastic tablecloths with pictures of watermelons, apples, and cherries, he noticed, trying to keep his head down. Once, when he was little, Gram had spread a cloth like these out for a picnic. They had taken turns pretending to pick a piece of fruit and eat it right off the cloth. How he wished he could grab a bunch of cherries off the plastic right now.

In the back of the café was a display case that held pastries: doughnuts, éclairs, croissants, giant muffins. A yeasty bread smell, combined with the scent of coffee, nearly overtook him, and for a moment he imagined grabbing a chocolate croissant off a woman's plate and bolting outside.

Instead, he looked around the side of the display case, toward the back of the shop, for a computer.

There wasn't one. How could this be a free-Internet café and not have a computer? On the wall he saw a small handwritten sign: WI-FI AREA. Oh, so you could have free Internet *if* you brought your own laptop. *Figures!* All the excitement he'd felt only moments ago leached out of him.

"You're him!" He turned at the loud whisper. It was the girl he'd met on the street—again standing so close, he could count the freckles on her nose. She'd been following him!

"You're the missing kid," she gasped.

Jack felt like a kid in a game of tag, about to be marked *it.* He couldn't catch his breath. He didn't know what to say, couldn't think. He pivoted from his left foot to his right and then ran, squeezing past tables and through crowds and out of the shop.

"Hey!" he heard her yell from behind him.

Jack sprinted past the rest of the storefronts on the block and down a side street before he paused to look over his shoulder. The girl was following him, and man, was she fast! There were no other roads shooting off the one he was on, and if his sense of direction was correct, this street would soon end at the ocean. Then what? A dog barked loudly, discouraging him from cutting across the unknown backyards. Instead, he suddenly reversed direction, clipping the girl with as much force as he could as he raced back up the hill, to the center of town, and ducked into a bookstore on the corner. A bell over the door jingled.

It was a smaller store than Jack expected, and, even though he could see instantly that it had lots of little nooks and crannies for sitting and reading, he knew he couldn't hide in there for long. Fortunately, the one and only customer in the store — a man who rocked back and forth on his heels as he spoke — was trying to explain his needs to a woman behind the counter. Jack moved to a back corner of the store, which happened to be the children's section, and sat for a moment in a small stuffed red chair to catch his breath.

He picked up a nearby graphic novel, hoping to look engrossed and be somewhat hidden if anyone else came into the store. He felt as if the girl's shout and his tearing out of the coffee shop so quickly had alerted everyone to the fact that something unusual was happening in town.

And no doubt he'd made the girl mad when he'd clipped her. Come to think of it, that was pretty stupid. She'd probably gone straight to the police station to report her sighting.

The woman came out from behind the counter and led the man to some shelves at the front of the store. "We could put the display here," she said.

Jack glanced around the bookshop for a rear exit. There was a curtained doorway in the back, but he doubted it led anywhere except to a closet-size office. But across from the counter was a partially open door—a heavy metal door. He decided to risk it. He could simply say he was confused if it led to a dead end.

Making as little noise as possible, he slipped through the open door and into . . . into what? What was this? There were boxes of books all around, but he was not in a typical storage room. Jack touched the walls—metal, too. He was in a . . . in a safe. Not a safe, a vault. The kind that he'd seen in a movie about notorious bank robbers. Why would there be a vault in a bookstore?

He read the label on one of the boxes: *Left Bank Books.* Maybe the store used to be a bank?

He was about to exit the vault when the light from outside was blocked. The girl from the café was standing three feet away, peering inside. He froze against the wall, hoping she wouldn't notice him in the shadows.

"Hello?" she called hesitantly.

His breath caught. Could she see him?

"Mrs. Magillicutty?"

That must be the woman who was behind the counter when he came in. So she couldn't see him! He wanted to exhale in relief, but he was afraid even the slightest movement would give him away.

As the girl continued to peer into the vault, Jack could hear the woman — Mrs. Magillicutty — at the front of the store. *Please go away,* Jack thought at the girl. *Please!*

The girl poked her head back outside the vault. "Mrs. M., have you seen — ?"

She was going to ask about him! And this would be the first place they'd look. He couldn't let that happen!

Not knowing what else to do, Jack reached out,

grabbed the girl's wrist, and pulled her into the vault with him.

"Ouch!" the girl cried, and then opened her mouth to yell.

Quickly, Jack pulled the door of the vault shut.

"What'd you do that for?" the girl shouted. "We're locked in here now, you know. And it's no use yelling. The Morris twins did that for hours, but no one heard them."

Jack couldn't see the girl's face in the dark, and so he stammered in her general direction. "Y-you were going to turn me in!"

"Of course I was going to turn you in. The whole state of Maine's looking for you! Your poor grandmother is worried sick."

He bristled at that but was glad she couldn't see it. "I can't let you turn me in," he said.

"But why? What'd you *do*?" The girl pulled her cell phone out of her bag and flipped it open. "I'd better get reception in here. I have a test this afternoon."

Jack couldn't even remember a time when his biggest worry was some test at school. "I didn't do anything."

The girl looked up from the screen. "Then why'd you run away?"

Where would he even start? he wondered. Not that he was actually going to tell this girl anything.

"I can't believe this. Not even a single bar!" She snapped her phone closed in frustration. "I wonder if Mrs. M. will hear us if we bang on the walls."

The thought of being discovered sent Jack's heart racing. "Couldn't you just pretend you locked yourself in by accident? I mean, when she realizes there's someone in here? I could hide in the shadows and slip out once the coast was clear."

"Slip out?" He could hear her sit down on a box. "You've got to be kidding. First of all, there's no telling how long it'll take for us to be discovered. We could be in here all day! Secondly, when we *are* discovered, Mrs. M. will be furious, and that's *nothing* compared to what will happen if anyone finds out I let you go."

"But no one would have to know you ever saw me. Like I said, I could just slip—"

"Slip out, I know. But how am I going to explain how I ended up in this vault in the first place without mentioning that I was following you? Besides, if I turn you in, I'll be a hero. And if I don't, and someone finds out about it—which they will—I'll probably be grounded for the rest of eighth grade."

Jack sat down on a box as well. His legs no longer felt like they could hold him. *"Please,"* he said. "I know turning me in seems like the right thing to do, but sometimes things aren't what they seem."

"Well, why don't you enlighten me, then?"

"Huh?"

"Convince me that I'm wrong. And everybody who's out looking for you, everybody in the state of Maine and your grandma and the police— convince me that we're all wrong, and that you're better off on your own."

Jack wrapped his good hand around the plastic elephant in his pocket. All of his instincts were telling him not to trust this strange girl, not to let her get any closer than she already was. But he felt trapped, cornered. What choice did he have, really?

"I don't even know you. . . ." he began, but he knew he was just stalling.

"Sylvie Winters," she said. "Nice to meet you. I don't remember if they mentioned your name on the news. . . ."

"I'm Jack," he said, and left it at that. He took a deep breath. "The reason you can't tell anybody is because if you do, I'll be . . ."

He could feel her staring at him, waiting.

Just like that, all the fight drained out of him. He put his head in his hands. "I'll be taken away from my mother," he whispered.

Sylvie was silent for a moment more and then asked, "Because she left? That's what happened, isn't it?"

Jack nodded.

"Permanently?" Sylvie asked.

His head snapped up. "No! She's gonna come back, I know she will. I just don't know how long she'll be gone."

"OK, OK. I believe you," Sylvie said, soothingly. "But what I meant was, do you think they would take you away from her permanently?"

Jack was glad for the darkness. It was easier to talk to her when she couldn't see him. "I don't know," he said. "But it's bad, right? I mean, could she go to jail for something like this?"

She paused. "I suppose," she said, as gently as

anyone could say such a thing. "I think it qualifies as abandonment or child neglect or something." He could tell she was thinking. "So, what were you planning on doing?"

"Before I got locked in a vault?" Jack asked.

Sylvie laughed. "Yeah. Before that."

He looked up. "I was going to see an elephant."

Twenty

It is known that one elephant who was rather slow in learning his tricks and had been punished severely by his master's beating, was discovered later that night, alone in his tent, practicing those tricks.
— PLINY THE ELDER, *NATURAL HISTORY,* BOOK III

"Would you like half of my sandwich?" Sylvie asked. They'd been trapped in the vault for at least two hours. "Or maybe we should each eat a quarter. Who knows how long we'll be in here."

Jack eagerly accepted and popped the entire portion of the egg-salad sandwich into his mouth before wishing he'd savored it.

"So, tell me another elephant story," said Sylvie.

He gave himself a moment to finish chewing and asked, "Aren't you tired of them?" though he was hardly tired of telling them. When Sylvie had questioned him about his determination to see Lydia, Jack had tried to explain his obsession with elephants by telling her some of the most amazing elephant stories and facts that he knew. He didn't think he'd convinced her not to turn him in, but he *had* convinced her that elephants were pretty darned cool.

"Well, then, tell me how you were planning to get all the way to York," Sylvie said.

"I don't know. Walk, I guess. I've gotten this far." Jack took off the hat he'd found. It had grown increasingly warm in the vault.

"Yeah, but *everyone* is looking for you now," said Sylvie. "It's all anyone wants to talk about . . . the missing boy."

"Really?" Jack found it hard to believe that there wouldn't be more important things to talk about—more important people to pursue—in Maine. Certainly, the state must have had its share of murders and burglaries, too.

"You've got to admit, it's a pretty gripping story. An eleven-year-old kid, all on his own, has somehow survived without any food or money or help. Plus, it's just driving people crazy that the entire

Maine state-police force hasn't found you yet. But I did," Sylvie added with a good deal of satisfaction.

Jack declined her offer of some grapes, even though he'd eaten very little. He had to face the fact that at some point, this vault was going to be opened and Sylvie was going to announce to the world that she had found the missing boy. He'd be carted off, his grandmother would be called, and all the struggles of the week would have been for naught. In fact, maybe he'd be in a whole heap of trouble for not having gone to an adult—not to mention for stealing the elephant and the bike. Maybe he and his mom would *both* be going to jail.

But if he could just hold on a little longer, just make it as far as York's Wild Kingdom, maybe by then everything would be OK. Maybe all he needed was to look into Lydia's eyes, and he'd know what was supposed to come next, how this would all work out. He couldn't give up now, not when he was so close.

Jack cleared his throat, not quite sure where his thoughts were going. "If you knew that you were going to be taken away from your mother, if you

knew you'd never live with her again, is there anything you'd like to do first?"

Sylvie checked her cell reception again. She'd
done it about fifteen times, even though there was
never a signal.

"I don't know," she said.

Jack pulled his fingers through his hair. If he
couldn't even get her to put herself in his shoes,
how would he ever convince her to let him go?

"I'd play Monopoly with her," Sylvie said
finally.

"Monopoly?"

"My mom is always trying to get me to play
board games with her—especially Monopoly. But
it's so boring, you know? Except, there are some
things I like. I like that my mom always tries to
land on Indiana Avenue because she went to school
in Indiana. And she always licks her finger twice
before picking up a Chance card. And she always
has to have the shoe."

"That's my mom's favorite, too."

"So, yeah, Monopoly. That's the last thing I'd
want to do with her before I left."

Jack wished his one last thing could be something he did with his mom and not something he had to do on his own. But he knew, deep down, that even if he was alone, seeing Lydia would be his Monopoly.

Sylvie offered the grapes again.

"*Mudo*," Jack said. He put one in his mouth and sucked on it slowly.

"*Mudo?*" asked Sylvie.

"It means 'thank you.'"

"Huh," said Sylvie. "So, seeing the elephant, seeing Lydia, really means that much to you?"

Jack nodded. "It's all I have left."

"But your mom—"

Suddenly, there was a clicking noise.

"The lock!" whispered Sylvie. He'd expected her to sound relieved, but instead she sounded frightened. "Mrs. M.'s opening the lock."

Jack held his breath, praying that she finally understood.

"Hide!" Sylvie commanded, pulling him toward a stack of boxes behind her.

Hope surged through him. Was she really—?

"Hide!" she said again.

Jack did as he was told and hid behind the pile of boxes—

And not a moment too soon. The heavy vault door swung open.

"Hi, Mrs. Magillicutty!"

"Good heavens!" Mrs. Magillicutty screeched. "Sylvie Winters, what on *earth* are you doing in here? You scared me half to death! How long—?"

"I came in this morning, looking for you, Mrs. M. I was checking to see if you were in here, and someone shut the door."

"What do you mean, *someone* shut the door? I never shut this door. . . . The sales rep, maybe? Or one of the customers? They should all know better. . . . Someday, someone is going to make me permanently close this vault," she muttered. Then she seemed to remember that Sylvie was there. "You're all right, though, sweetie, aren't you?"

"I'm fine, Mrs. M. Just happy to be free!"

Jack wondered if that last bit was for his benefit. Maybe she really *did* understand.

"What did you need me for in the first place?"

Mrs. Magillicutty asked. Her voice sounded farther away, like maybe Sylvie was leading her to the front of the store.

"It was just a silly question about a book. I can't even remember what it was, exactly," said Sylvie, who was definitely farther away. "But, Mrs. M., can you take me to school and help explain? I have a test this afternoon. . . ."

Twenty-one

*In Thailand, people walk under
an elephant's belly for luck.*

Jack waited until he heard the bell jingle over the
door, until he could no longer hear Sylvie's voice.
Then he slid out from behind the boxes, went
directly to the front door of the store, turned the
lock, and slipped out into the sunshine.

If what Sylvie had said was true—that *everyone*
was looking for him—he had to hide immediately. He turned sharply to the left and headed back
down behind the buildings on Main Street, following the same route he'd attempted earlier, when
Sylvie was chasing him. He knew he shouldn't stay

on the street—not when every kid in Searsport was in school—but where to hide?

Several of the houses on this street had garages, and one or two had a shed. *Just pick one,* he told himself, *before an old lady looks out her window and calls the police.* But he couldn't bring himself to do it. Maybe it was because he'd been trapped in a vault for the past three hours, but hiding out in another confining space was the last thing he wanted to do right now.

The road he was on quickly led to a park— MOSMAN PARK, the sign read—and, although the park was pretty deserted at this hour except for a dog walker in the distance, it was wide open, with no apparent places to hide. Jack continued down to the shore and followed a rock beach, similar to the one he'd seen in Bar Harbor, along the coastline.

He could see sailboats in the distance, and lobster boats. *Maybe,* he thought, *I could hide away on one of those. Travel by boat to York instead of walking.* But so far, his one attempt at stowing away had not exactly been successful. With his luck, he'd end up docking in Canada, and, although he might avoid being arrested, the likelihood of seeing his mother again, he figured, would be much slimmer.

There was a seawall that lined the beach, and lobster traps were piled along it. Jack crawled behind the bank of lobster traps and plunked down. It was the perfect hiding spot—cozy and well concealed—and yet he could still look out at the sea. *I'll wait here until dark,* he decided, *then I'll start walking to York.* He'd have to be careful and duck whenever a car came into view, but if no one spotted him walking, he could make it pretty far overnight.

He dug around in the sand a bit, looking for shell fragments, and figured it was getting close to noon. Noon would mean midday hunger pangs. But he was learning that if he just ignored them, they would lessen in an hour or so. It was strange; hunger was like an alarm clock. It sounded for a while, but if you ignored it, it would eventually give up. The alarm would go off again around dinnertime, he knew, but he'd deal with that when the time came.

Sudden noises startled Jack: women's voices and the easily recognizable sound of dog tags. *Please let the dog be on a leash,* thought Jack. If not, the dog would surely sniff him out, and there was no way he could convince the women that he was a home-schooled kid just hiding behind some lobster traps.

"Waldo!" shouted a woman. "Stop it!"

The dog drew nearer. He was big and black and, luckily, leashed. But he was barking and lunging at the lobster traps, and, although Jack could see the owner only from the waist down, he could tell that the dog was succeeding in pulling her closer.

"Do you think there's an animal hiding back there?" asked the other woman, whose voice was calmer, deeper.

Jack tried to disappear into the wall behind him.

"What, like a seal? Whoa, Waldo! Cut it out! A seal would be sweet."

"I was thinking a squirrel, or a cat from one of the houses around here."

"Waldo, come!"

The dog immediately stopped lunging at the traps and began bouncing against the woman's leg.

"He knows *that* command!" said the woman with the deeper voice.

"He knows that obeying it means a cookie," said the owner. She gave the dog a treat, and the three of them moved on.

Jack let out his breath. He was lucky, but he wasn't going to stay here. The next dog might be off leash, and not nearly as fond of Milk-Bones as this one.

He gave up on the beach and headed back into a nearby neighborhood, where he took a closer look at the toolsheds and garages. It wasn't ideal, but it sure beat being sniffed out by a curious dog.

Before long, he found an open toolshed in the corner of a backyard. The shed mostly contained gardening equipment: plastic pots and bags of soil, clippers and rakes. But in the corner was a faded director's chair, and next to the chair was a plastic bin filled with dingy mystery magazines from the 1970s. As Jack squeezed past the lawn mower and into the chair, he wondered about the person who escaped to this shed to do a little reading. He decided to move the chair to the one and only window, which gave him a view of the house—and, he hoped, of anyone approaching.

He read for hours, thankful for the distraction. Once, just after he'd finished a story about a man whose wife had disappeared, Jack heard the back door of the house open. A woman came out and sat for a while on her back step. That was all. She just sat, turning her face toward the sun. Then she got up and went back inside.

Another time, Jack saw a couple of little kids running across the yard. They seemed like they were in a hurry to get somewhere—maybe down to the beach—and they sure didn't notice him sitting by the window of the shed. But if they had, wouldn't that have made the beginning of a great mystery?

Jack read till the shed grew dark and his eyes hurt. Finally, he felt it was late enough, safe enough, to begin traveling.

He headed up the road as if he lived in this neighborhood, as if he was a boy who belonged and who had someplace to go. To his surprise, he felt most comfortable while walking down Main Street. After all, would a kid who was on the lam (as the writers of mysteries liked to say) walk boldly through town? It wasn't until he'd gone beyond the center and was back on the rural roads that he felt conspicuous. He was glad for the cap then.

For the most part, it was easy to spot cars coming from the opposite direction and to duck out of sight, whether by standing behind a tree, diving into a ditch, or crouching behind some bushes. But not so when he neared the top of a hill or when cars came up from behind him.

That was why, even after two hours of trying to be careful, to stay focused and to frequently look back as he walked, he didn't see the van until it was practically on top of him. He scrambled up the bank and into the trees, but the van slowed—and then rolled to a stop.

Twenty-two

It was once assumed that all elephants in a group were related. But not so. If an elephant family has been torn apart due to poaching, elephants will form new families.

The driver's door opened.

Jack spun and ran but immediately tripped over a root and flew face-first to the ground. He used his hands to try to break the fall and wrenched his broken finger. The pain rocketed up his arm, distracting him from the stinging of his torn-up face.

"Jack!" he heard a young-sounding guy yell—a guy who was approaching quickly. A guy who must have watched the news, who knew who he was, knew about his grandmother and his mom, and who knew what else?

Jack stayed perfectly still, hoping that he wouldn't be seen on the ground.

"Jack! I'm here to help. I'm Wyatt. Sylvie's cousin!"

Sylvie's cousin? Was it possible . . . ?

"I'll take you to York!"

York! So he really did know Sylvie.

"Jack!" the guy bellowed. It was clear that he thought Jack had run off into the woods, that he had no idea Jack was lying on the ground just a few feet away. Jack could stay right where he was and the guy would probably give up. But what if he really did want to help? What if he was willing to drive Jack all the way to York tonight? No more hiding out, no more walking along the highway at night, no more leaping into bushes and taking face-plants in the dirt. He'd see Lydia tomorrow.

But could he trust him?

"Jack!" the guy yelled again.

He'd trusted Nina, and look where that had gotten him. But what were his choices? Spend days hiding and nights walking—or get a ride now?

"I'm right here," said Jack.

"Whoa!" Wyatt was clearly surprised to hear

Jack's voice come out of the dark. "Geez, man, I didn't see you. You can't go scaring people like that. You nearly gave me a heart attack."

"Are you really Sylvie's cousin?" Jack asked, standing, adjusting the splint on his throbbing finger, and trying, with his good hand, to brush off the sticks and leaves that had adhered to his bare legs.

"Yup." Wyatt—a teenager, Jack could now see—turned and walked back to the road, seeming confident that Jack would follow. "She told me about your little adventure today. I used to be scared to death of getting locked in that safe."

"So how did you know to come looking for me now?" Jack asked, hopping up into the passenger seat of the ancient van and taking a good look at Sylvie's cousin. Jack figured he was only a couple of years older than Sylvie. He was tall, and kind of skinny, and probably hadn't had his license for very long.

"I didn't even know about you until a half hour ago. Sylvie called me—she was crazed . . . thought you might have waited till dark to travel and was imagining all sorts of creepy consequences."

Jack was relieved to hear that not *everyone* in Maine knew about him and was looking for him. "Yeah, well, thanks for picking me up. And for taking me to York." He didn't know whether Sylvie had mentioned why he was so determined to get to York, and he decided not to bring it up now. Telling Sylvie was one thing; telling this high-school kid, who was likely to think he was ridiculous, was another.

Wyatt started up the van and, with hardly a glance in the rearview mirror, screeched onto the highway. Jack reached over and grabbed the seat belt he'd yet to buckle, clicking it into place just as they barreled around a sharp corner.

"How long will it take us to get there?" Jack asked.

Wyatt seemed to be doing calculations in his head, which probably meant that he hadn't *really* imagined himself traveling all the way to southern Maine tonight. "Route Three is up ahead. . . . That's the fastest, I think."

"I was trying to avoid the turnpike," Jack said, as a way of making small talk. "That's why I was taking Route One."

"What—why? You think there're roadblocks on the turnpike or something?"

"Well, actually, I was just—"

"Hey, man. I thought Sylvie was exaggerating. Just being melodramatic, as usual. But the Staties—they're *really* looking for you?"

Jack nodded, not sure whether this information would change things or not. "Yeah, I guess I've been on the news a lot."

"Cool," said the kid, whose left leg started jangling like he was nervous. He bypassed the exit for Route 3, probably thinking it was too dangerous. Jack wished he'd kept his big mouth shut; what if Wyatt was too nervous to take him all the way to York, now that he knew he was a fugitive?

They passed through a fairly busy town, and Jack fought the urge to duck down in his seat; he didn't want to scare Wyatt any more than he already had. They had just reached the town center when Wyatt's phone rang. He pulled it out of his pocket and glanced at the screen. "It's Sylvie," he said, and handed Jack his phone. "Talk to her."

"Hello?" Jack said.

"Wyatt?"

"No, this is Jack."

"Jack! You're OK! And Wyatt must have found you!"

"Yeah. Thanks for sending him."

"I kept thinking about you, all alone in the dark, trying to get to York. . . . Anyway, I just had to tell someone, and I knew Wyatt would agree to help you," Sylvie said in a rush. "I hope you're not mad."

"Mad? Are you kidding?" said Jack. "You were awesome at the bookstore. And I really appreciate Wyatt's help."

Before hanging up, he promised Sylvie two things: one, that he'd find a way to call her when he finally saw Lydia, and two, he'd never ever tell anyone that she and Wyatt were involved in helping him. "If my father didn't kill us, my uncle would," she said. "Just say you hitched or something."

Not long after Jack got off the phone with Sylvie, Wyatt started pummeling Jack with questions, each seeming a little weirder than the one before.

"How long have you been on your own?

"Where's the coolest place you've stayed?

"What's the grossest thing you had to eat?

"How did the cops learn about you?

"Where does your grandmother live?

"Is she loaded?"

It was this last question that seemed the strangest to Jack. Why would Wyatt think his grandmother was rich? Maybe he assumed that no one bothered to search for poor kids, or maybe he'd read too many books like *The Boxcar Children* or *The Great Gilly Hopkins,* where kids who'd been on their own ended up living with a rich relative. Jack wasn't sure how to answer. His grandmother wasn't filthy rich, but she lived in a big brick house in Cambridge, and she'd never worked—or at least, Jack had never known her to work. So Jack just mumbled something like, "Well, she is always offering to pay for lessons or take me on vacations," and let it go at that. He didn't bother adding that his mother would never have allowed his grandmother to pay for either.

"What I wouldn't do for a little money—a little independence," said Wyatt. "I'd live on the road like you, traipsing off to see wild elephants whenever I felt like it."

So Sylvie *had* told him. But Wyatt didn't seem to want to make fun of him.

Jack realized that getting trapped in the safe with Sylvie was probably one of the luckiest things that had happened to him that week. If he hadn't met Sylvie, Wyatt would not have come looking for him, and he wouldn't have gotten all the way to York's Wild Kingdom in one night. He wondered what he would do when they arrived. Would he find a place to hide until the park opened tomorrow? And how would he pay for admission? He'd been so busy thinking about *getting* to the animal park that he'd hardly thought about what he'd do once he got there (other than see Lydia, of course). Maybe he'd be better off trying to sneak in tonight. Jack pulled a hand through his very dirty hair. He was tired of thinking. He'd figure it out when he got there, just as he'd figured out everything else on this trip so far.

And he was starving. Unfortunately, they'd already passed through two towns with drive-throughs, and now they were back on a stretch of deserted road with very few businesses of any kind.

"Wyatt?"

Jack's voice seemed to startle Wyatt out of a dream.

"Do you think I could borrow some money from you for food tonight? I promise I'll pay you back—send it to you—when I get back home."

"Or your grandmother could send it to me," said Wyatt.

"Yeah, maybe." He figured it wasn't worth trying to explain the grandmother situation.

"What do you want to eat?"

A Big Mac was the first thing that came to mind, but Jack doubted they'd find a McDonald's on this stretch.

"Anything," said Jack. "Maybe there's a store coming up. I'm sure I could find something."

"Yeah, that's the way to do it on the open road," said Wyatt. "Just stop and see what life brings you."

Yeah, life or the grocery truck, Jack thought, and instantly realized that that was what his mom would have said. He felt a burning in his chest and was grateful that they didn't have to travel far before Wyatt pulled into the parking lot of a Citgo station with a convenience store.

"Here's a ten. Let me know if you need more," said Wyatt as they were hopping out of the van.

"Thanks," said Jack. "I'm going to hit the men's room first." He entered the store and walked toward the back, keeping his head down and his cap pulled low.

He took one look at his bloody, scratched-up face in the mirror and wondered, *What was I thinking?* His face would definitely raise questions. He'd be stupid to try to buy something, especially since he was so close to getting to York. No. He'd figure out what he wanted and ask Wyatt to get it for him while he waited in the van.

He washed his face as gently as he could and then drank from the faucet.

As he left the restroom, Jack could hear Wyatt's voice. Dang! If Wyatt was talking to someone, it would be hard to get his attention unnoticed. Jack stayed where he was, in a deserted aisle next to the Cheerios and cornflakes, hoping that Wyatt wouldn't talk long.

"How far is York from Warren? Can you look it up?" Wyatt asked.

Jack listened for a response but didn't hear anything.

"Holy cow," Wyatt said.

He must be talking on his phone, Jack thought. Was he talking to Sylvie? He started toward Wyatt, planning to signal that he needed his attention.

"Search his name. See if his grandmother is offering a reward."

A *reward*? Dang! Was Wyatt going to turn him in? And if he was, would he wait until after they'd arrived in York? *Will he at least let me see the elephant first?*

"Right there," said a soft-spoken woman from somewhere behind him.

Jack looked up. There were round mirrors in the corners of the store. He moved forward until he could see two women behind the counter—one his mom's age, one a teenager—both staring at the same mirror. Could they see him? Suddenly, whether Wyatt was going to turn him in or not didn't matter anymore. He'd probably raised enough suspicion already, just standing frozen in the cereal aisle, to get himself caught. Jack casually backtracked to the entrance and bolted out the door.

Once Wyatt discovered he'd fled from the store, he probably wouldn't be able to resist telling others that Jack was the missing boy. Maybe he hoped they'd still give him the reward, if there even was one.

So, how far *was* York from Warren? Jack wished he'd heard the answer. He must have run a mile when he looked over his shoulder and spotted headlights. He immediately leaped into the brush on the side of the road. The thorny branches scratched his already battered face, and gravel dug into his knees. His finger throbbed worse than ever.

Crouched in that ditch, bruised and battered, Jack was overcome with despair. He was right back to where he was before Wyatt came along: traveling in the dark, hungry, tired, having to jump every time a car came. And, even though he knew he was closer to York, he didn't know how far he had yet to go. What if it was days?

Maybe he'd been too hasty in bolting. Maybe there was time to catch Wyatt before he started blabbing to the store clerks. He could eat something, try to persuade Wyatt to help him out—to turn him in *after* he got to York, at the very least.

He turned around and jogged back toward the store, still careful to duck out of sight whenever a car approached.

Finally, the convenience store came into view.

Jack's heart stopped.

A police car was parked outside.

He crouched in the shadow of a tree. It was too late to catch a ride with Wyatt. And he had no way of knowing how far he was from York. What if he just stopped running, just walked right up to the officer and said, "Hey, looking for me?" It would be so much easier. He'd get a hot meal, a shower, a bed. But then what? Would they arrest him for running away, for stealing the elephant and the bike and making everyone in the state of Maine look for him?

And they would have a lot of questions for him—but they wouldn't be the kind of questions Wyatt had asked. They'd be more along the lines of "Did your mother tell you she was leaving?" and "Has she ever left you before?" The problem with those questions was that he couldn't answer them truthfully without getting his mother deeper into trouble. He'd be the one sealing both of their fates. Nope, he still wasn't ready for that.

Next to the store, along a white fence, was a Dumpster. A place to hide. If the police were looking for him, they'd likely check around the store, in the woods, along the road. But it wasn't likely they'd check inside a Dumpster, was it?

Jack studied the scene carefully. He could see the police officer inside the store, talking to the two women who'd spotted him. There was no sign of Wyatt, though he could see the van parked where they'd left it. He imagined the police officer would be talking to Wyatt next.

There was no one else around. It was now or never.

Jack held his breath and dashed toward the Dumpster, crouching as low as possible. He quickly lifted the lid, hoping that the trash would be contained in plastic garbage bags and that it wouldn't smell too bad.

Fortunately, the Dumpster had just been emptied. There were loose paper bags, the kind that might hold a sandwich or a pastry, and paper cups with loose-fitting lids, tossed in by customers, but no large garbage bags—and no smell. Jack hoisted himself up and over, being careful of his broken pinky and trying not to make any noise.

The Dumpster was heavy-duty plastic, so he could move around quietly. He took a moment before settling down to look inside the bags. Most were empty, but one held a cruller with a single bite taken out of it. It was stale—he could tell by how crumbly it was—but who was he to be picky? And another contained a half-eaten bag of potato chips. Score! He sat in one of the back corners of the Dumpster, wolfing down the food, and marveled at his brilliance. He was hidden, had something to eat, and could easily peek out the top of the Dumpster to see if Wyatt or the police had left yet.

Flashing lights alerted Jack to the fact that more police cars had arrived. Jack peeked out and saw Wyatt talking to a police officer, who was writing things down, but Jack was too far away to hear what he was saying. Was he lying, saying he hadn't seen a kid in the store? Or was he telling the police officer everything, including that he, Jack Martel, was determined to get to York's Wild Kingdom?

If he did manage to make it to the animal park, would the whole State of Maine police force be waiting for him there?

After what seemed like an eternity, Jack watched Wyatt get in his van and head back the way they'd come. Then, one by one, the police cars began to leave. Two headed down Route 1 in the direction that Jack needed to go.

Two remaining police officers, both with coffee cups in hand, began to approach the Dumpster. Jack backed away into one of the far corners and curled himself into the smallest shape possible.

"So, the kid knew nothing?"

"Nope. Apparently he got it in his head that he'd be the one to find the Martel kid tonight. Said he was searching the roads."

"Does he have information we don't?"

"I don't see how he could. I think he just got lucky—happened to pull into the gas station right at the time the Martel kid needed to use the toilet. . . ."

So Wyatt hadn't told. Maybe he was still holding out for the reward. If so, Jack wondered if Wyatt would come back looking for him later that night. Another reason to stay off the road tonight.

Or maybe Wyatt was doing him a favor. Maybe he wasn't so different from Sylvie, after all. . . .

One of the officers lifted the lid of the Dumpster, and two cups of lukewarm coffee came splashing down on Jack.

Twenty-three

When you have got an elephant by
the hind leg and he is trying to run
away, it's best to let him run."
— ABRAHAM LINCOLN

Jack waited awhile longer; then he slipped out of the Dumpster and jumped over the fence to see what was behind the store. There he found an old, turquoise car, the kind of old car that people love to shine up and drive in parades; only this one was missing its tires and had rust around its doors. The backseat proved the perfect place to spend the night. (Even though Jack knew he was probably sharing the seat with a mouse or two.)

He woke just before the sun rose and figured that only truck drivers would be out this early. And truck drivers were mostly from out of state; they probably wouldn't have heard of him. If he started walking now, he wouldn't need to do so much walking and hiding at night.

After walking for about an hour, seeing practically nothing but trees (and he was right—only two trucks and one car had passed him), he came to a fork. He had a choice between Route 1 and Old Route 1. He took Old Route 1, figuring it went in the same direction but might have fewer vehicles as it started to get later.

At first, this road, too, was nothing but trees, but after another hour or so had passed, the road began to be at first spotted and then lined with houses. It was obvious he was approaching a town, and he figured he should start looking for a place to hide during daylight. He passed one house with a sign advertising a room for rent (he wished he could borrow it for a day!) and another advertising violin lessons (something he'd never been tempted to try). He kept his eyes out for garages or sheds.

He passed a few houses without any luck. He was just starting to get anxious, when a thought struck:

it was Saturday. That might give him another hour of traveling time, since most people tended to stay at home this early on Saturday mornings. Maybe he'd try just getting through this town and seeing what was on the other side.

The sun was warm on his head and shoulders, but not too hot. And the sky was a clear, bright blue. It reminded Jack of fall days when he used to play elephant in the park near his home. He would be romping around, imagining, and the world around him would come into sharper focus . . . and at the same time almost disappear. There was a feeling of joy in those moments, of peace. He felt that way now and walked a little bit taller. He was going to make it to York. He could feel it.

He had just reached the tiny, run-down, and rather deserted town center, another strip of connected brick storefronts, when a black car with a blue stripe — a police cruiser — suddenly pulled up beside him. He should have ducked into a shed when he'd had the chance!

Jack pushed his hand with the broken finger into his pocket and tried to breathe normally.

"Hey, son," the officer said as Jack tried to walk on by.

Jack glanced up, just enough to see the blue uniform, the badge.

Fear pulsed through his body. Every instinct screamed at him to run, but he didn't dare; he'd never outrun the cruiser. But he couldn't ignore the policeman, either. Not without arousing suspicion.

But how would he explain all the scrapes on his face?

"Hello," he said, turning to face the officer but keeping his head tipped down.

"Do you live here in town?" the officer asked.

"Yes," Jack said. *Oh, that was brilliant. Obviously, the next question will be, where?* "I have a violin lesson in a half hour," said Jack. "Just killing time."

"Oh yeah? What's your violin teacher's name?"

"Um, Mrs.—" He banged his head with his left hand and tried to look scatterbrained. "I can't believe I'm forgetting it. I only started last week. But her house is right down there," he said, pointing toward the house he'd passed with the violin-lessons sign.

"So, where's your violin?"

Jack's palms started sweating. He could tell the officer didn't believe him. "I'm borrowing one. My parents want to make sure I stick with it before they buy me one." Which was exactly what his mom *had* said when he begged to take up the trumpet last year.

"Well, why don't you get in? I'll drive you to your lesson."

"That's OK. It's not that far," he said. "Anyway, I wanted to get some breakfast first."

"OK," said the officer. "Just wanted to be of help."

"Thanks, though," Jack said, figuring that's what a normal kid would do in this situation. His heart still hammering away, he turned and started to walk toward the nearest store, which appeared to be a drugstore.

"Hey, Jack!" the officer yelled.

Jack turned around. "Yeah?"

And then he realized what he'd done.

He'd fallen for a trick—answered to his own name!

"Thought so," said the officer calmly. "Get in the car, son. I'll take you to Moody's Diner for breakfast—after we radio news to your grand-mother."

The world was collapsing around Jack. He'd come so far. He'd tried so hard! And he'd been so close! But he'd let everyone down—his mother (who would probably go to jail now), and Sylvie, and even Wyatt, who would likely be in big trouble for lying to the police.

Suddenly, he was running, even though he knew it was pointless. He heard the police officer calling after him but didn't dare stop. He ducked into the drugstore, which seemed to be empty, and ran toward the back, praying there would be a door. There was. He flew through the door and came to a stairwell. Up or down? Down was darker. He raced down the stairs into a dark, crowded base-ment. Small windows let in just enough light for him to see a door in the back. He ran to the door and searched frantically for the knob. There wasn't one. Or even a latch.

The door was nailed shut.

He was trapped.

Jack crouched between a broken wheelchair and cardboard boxes full of cartons of cotton swabs.

He could hear feet pounding on the old wooden floors above. Voices called out for him: the booming voice of the police officer, and a softer voice — the voice of the pharmacist, Jack guessed.

At one point, the policeman came into the basement and flicked on a dim light. He also used his flashlight — shining it into all the corners. Jack had never remained so still in his entire life. In fact, if he hadn't felt his heart madly searching for a way to exit his body, he would have sworn he was dead.

"No kid would stay down here very long," the cop called up.

"I keep meaning to clean it up."

"Is this your only exit?" asked the policeman, slowly ascending the steps.

"There's a fire escape at the other end of the building. I've got a floor plan in the office I can show you."

Jack hadn't seen an office. Had he missed a door? His only hope now was that it would look like he'd gone down that fire escape. But he doubted it would be that simple.

Jack shivered uncontrollably, his muscles exhausted from holding still so long.

He could still hear voices above him, but he could no longer hear what was being said. He figured his best bet would be to do exactly what he'd done at L.L. Bean: stay put until the store closed and hope that by that time, the police would have assumed he was long gone.

He straightened his legs, trying not to think of the bazillion spiders that must be all around him.

The basement smelled like a combination of mold and cat litter. He tried to distract himself with his elephant, but it was too dark to see it. He could only hold it, taking comfort from the familiar shape of it.

Jack wondered if this was what it would feel like to live alone in his apartment, waiting for his mother to return—or for someone to catch onto him. First, someone would turn off the electricity, then the phone. Those companies didn't fool around—Jack knew. Once, during a spinning time, his mom had forgotten to pay the bills, and little by little everything stopped working. She had forgotten to pay the rent, too, but their landlady had given them an extra month before coming to collect. It probably helped that Jack had been the one to speak to her.

Man, he hated thinking about those things! And he hated sitting here, waiting to be caught. Because he knew the likelihood of everyone assuming he'd slipped out of the store unnoticed was slim to none. If he had to be caught, he'd rather be caught running than just sitting here waiting.

From the sounds of the infrequent footsteps above, the drugstore was not very busy. And he could no longer hear the police officer and the pharmacist talking. He hoped that the cop had gone back out to his cruiser and that the pharmacist had gone back to his counter.

He decided he'd try to find the fire escape. It was probably on the second floor. He crept back up the stairs. Each time a stair creaked, he stopped and waited, holding his breath.

But no one came.

When Jack got back to the landing, he took time to check things out. The door straight ahead of him would lead him back into the store. He looked to the right. Ah, there was the office. The door was slightly ajar. Two boots, crossed at the ankles, were resting on the desktop.

The police officer was right there.

The officer's voice came from the office. "I've called for reinforcements. Officers are searching the area, but I think he's still in the store. I'm going to wait it out, see if he shows himself when he gets hungry enough."

Dang. That meant there were likely police cars parked outside the front door. He wondered what the odds were of there not being any by the fire escape—if he could even find the fire escape.

To the left of the office was another flight of stairs. What was up there? More offices? Storage? The fire escape? What if the cop heard his footsteps? What if there were no places to hide?

Maybe it would be smarter to go back down into the basement, where at least it was dark. But how long would it be before the officer became frustrated and headed back down to search again?

If he went up, he just might find that fire escape.

But would someone be waiting at the bottom for him?

He wished he had his cell phone, wished he could call Nina and ask her what he should do.

The thought startled him. Why would he want to call the very person who'd exposed him in the first place? But he had to admit: it was *her* voice he wanted to hear at the end of the telephone line right now.

He reached into his pocket and pulled out the little elephant. *What should I do?* The elephant didn't say a word, but its mouth seemed to be smiling beneath its raised trunk. He remembered his teacher's words: "A trunk pointing up means good luck." *Good luck,* thought Jack. He'd follow that trunk and go up!

He set one foot on the first stair and gradually rested his weight on it, ready to jump back if there was a squeak. Nothing. He tested the next step. There was a bit of a groan from the wood, but not one loud enough to alert the policeman, who was still talking. Up he went in this way, testing a step, waiting. Testing a step, waiting.

On the second floor was a hallway with only a single door to the left. There was a little whiteboard on the door where someone had written, *I came by. Where were you?* A pair of flip-flops and an umbrella stand holding a green umbrella were in the corner. He guessed there was an apartment behind that door. He crept past the door and climbed to the third floor.

The third floor was a wide-open space with mirrors on one wall and a line of chairs on the opposite. *A dance studio,* Jack thought. He tiptoed across the floor to see what was behind an open door. Just then, he saw movement from the corner of his eye—he wasn't alone!

He spun around, and the figure spun around, too. It was only his reflection in the mirrors. He waited till the panic stopped ringing in his ears and then completed the slow trek across the floor.

A bathroom. There was a small bathroom behind the door. Where was the fire escape? He crept over to the large windows, standing off to the side so that he wouldn't be seen. There was a police car parked in front of the store, just as he'd suspected. But only one. Maybe that was what counted as backup around here.

Perhaps they hadn't even bothered guarding the rear exit.

He padded over to the windows on the side of the building. It was hard to see what was below without moving right up to the glass. Yes! There was a wrought-iron fire escape off this window, and no police car below—or any other cars or people, really, except for one red pickup truck, parked on a hill below.

Jack carefully opened the window and tried to yank off the screen. At first, the springs wouldn't budge; then one gave loose. The other followed suddenly, causing the screen to fly out of his hands and clatter against the metal fire escape.

Dang it! So much for a quiet getaway!

Jack climbed out the window and scrambled down the metal steps, no longer caring how much noise he made. He was thinking only about going fast enough to escape yet slowly enough to not careen off the side and smash his skull on the street below. *Left, right, left, right*—by concentrating on the steps this way, he'd reach the bottom safely.

He could see that the stairs didn't go all the way to the ground and that at some point, he'd have to jump. He reminded himself to keep his injured finger out of the way this time and to roll with the force if he needed to.

He hit the final step and leaped off, hoping that the landing would be soft and that he could keep right on moving, racing far away from here.

Jack's feet hit the grass and his knees buckled,

but he managed to keep himself upright. He had just pushed off again when he was grabbed from behind and jerked back.

He tried to thrash his arms, but two much larger arms had pinned them down. So he kicked, kicked hard. He had to get free, had to keep going . . . !

The arms held tight. And Jack knew it was useless. He'd been caught. It was over.

He couldn't believe it! After all he'd been through, trying so hard to keep his mother's disappearance a secret. To keep her from getting in trouble. And he'd been so close to his goal, to doing the one thing that would tell her it was all OK. That he still loved her, no matter what.

With a heartbroken sob, Jack gave up. He stopped kicking. He stopped struggling. He just went limp.

"So, how's the finger, kid?"

He knew that voice!

It wasn't a cop! It was Big Jack!

Big Jack must have sensed the change in Jack. He loosened his hold, and Jack whipped around and hugged him round the middle.

"What are you doing here?" Jack blurted.

"Looking for you, that's what. I can't tell you how relieved I was when I got a call telling me they'd found you."

Jack backed up. Big Jack was working with the police? He should have known he was just one more adult trying to trap him! To keep him from doing the one thing in the world he needed to do right now!

Jack glanced down the hill. Big Jack was, well, *big*. If he took off now, he could probably out-run him.

"Hey, talk to me. I'm not a bad guy. I can help," Big Jack said in a real calm voice, like the kind you use with trapped animals.

"You're not going to help," said Jack, inching backward. "You're just trying to turn me over to DSS like everyone else."

"I'm just trying to do what's best for you," said Big Jack.

"What *you* think is best for me," Jack countered. "No one cares about what *I* want."

"Well, for starters," said Big Jack, "I think you want to talk to your mom."

Jack stared at the ground. "But nobody even

knows where she is," he mumbled. "Except somewhere between here and the Bahamas."

"Actually, we do. Officer Kline tracked her down this morning. She's eager to talk to you."

Jack's ears began to ring again. They'd found his mom! She was OK!

All this time he'd spent wondering if she was all right, if he would ever get to talk to her again. And now he knew. He should be happy. So why did he feel like screaming?

"Jack?" Big Jack said.

Jack turned away and burst into tears. Sobbing, heaving, snot-dripping tears. He picked up a stone and threw it at a tree. Then another one. And another. "Why? Dang it! Why!" he sobbed.

Big Jack grabbed him and pulled him back into a hug.

Everything was flooding over Jack right now. Waking up at the campsite, all alone. The unanswered message he'd left on her cell phone. The days on the road, sleeping in the backs of trucks and in stores and churches. All the times he'd lied and stolen. All the people who'd been looking for him, worrying about him.

He was so ashamed.

Ashamed of it all, of everything that he'd done.

But most of all, ashamed because . . .

Because she'd left him.

There.

In between sobs, he thought it.

My mother . . .

My mother left me.

She

left

me.

Twenty-four

If the world held magic powerful enough to make the elephant appear, then there must exist, too, magic in equal measure, magic powerful enough to undo what had been done.
— KATE DICAMILLO, THE MAGICIAN'S ELEPHANT

Big Jack ushered him into his truck just moments before a police car passed by.

"It's not that I want to harbor a fugitive," said Big Jack. "But I want to give you a moment to catch your breath."

"And then what?" Jack mumbled, not really caring about the answer.

"Let's talk about it." Big Jack started his truck and pulled out.

Jack pulled his Searsport cap over his eyes.

"So, home is Boston, huh? Seems like you were pretty determined to get there on your own."

Jack shook his head.

"No?" asked Big Jack.

"No. Not really. . . . I was—" Jack sat up.

"Yeah?" said Big Jack. He drove slowly up and down the side streets of the little town, buying time.

"I was trying to get to the York wild-animal park," Jack blurted.

"Interesting. And why's that?"

"There's an elephant there," said Jack.

"Lydia?"

"You know her?"

"Sure, I grew up in southern Maine. But she's not there now. Her owners take her back to Florida after Labor Day."

"Labor Day?" Jack squeaked, his breath squeezed from his body.

It just wasn't possible, not after all his trying! It couldn't all have been for nothing!

"How would seeing an elephant help you, anyway?" Big Jack asked.

Jack tried to talk but had to stop himself a couple of times, knowing if he kept going, he was just going to cry again. Finally, he gulped air and said, "I can't explain it. But I just knew that if I made it there, if I saw Lydia, somehow everything would be all right."

"Hmmm." Big Jack was quiet for a moment. "You know, it isn't *that* long after Labor Day," he said. "Less than a week."

Hope fluttered in Jack's chest. He looked over at Big Jack. "Do you really think . . . ?"

Big Jack shrugged, but he was smiling. "Hand me my phone."

Big Jack called the wild-animal park and talked to someone in an office on speakerphone.

"Lydia? Oh, yeah, she's still here," the woman said.

Jack let out a whoop. He couldn't believe it!

"At least, she was here this morning. She's due to head south today, though. The truck might have left already."

"Is there some way you could find out for us?" Big Jack asked. The woman put them on hold while she called someone else. Jack held his breath till she came back on the line.

"I'm sorry, sir. No one's picking up."

Big Jack thanked her and hung up. "What do you think, kid? Is it worth a shot?"

"Yes!" Jack shouted. No *way* was he going to give up now, not while there was even the slightest hope of seeing Lydia.

Big Jack chuckled. "You remind me of me, kid. We'll try. But as soon as we get close to that park, I'm going to have to call someone. Both our butts are on the line now."

Big Jack stepped on the gas, and they raced onto the highway.

There was nothing but trees on both sides of the road, but that didn't keep Jack from staring out the window, watching them fly by.

"Tell me about your grandmother," said Big Jack after some time had passed. "Why didn't you call her?"

"She hates my mother."

"I don't want to contradict you—you knowing her and all. But I talked to her, and, well, that's not the impression I got. Your grandmother defended your mother. Said she's a *great* mom. Said your mother loves you like crazy. But she gets sick, right? From what I understand, she has an illness."

Jack nodded and started to cry again. Not the sobbing, retching crying he did earlier. Just tears, tears that seemed like they would never stop.

"Do you want to call your grandmother?"

Jack thought about the last time he'd seen his grandmother. He could picture his mother and his grandmother in her kitchen, yelling. Gram had said she was worried about him, said she wanted to help.

Mom had said Gram was evil, had insisted that Gram wanted to keep him, to take him away from her.

Then his mother had grabbed him by the hand and pulled him out of the house.

Mom was prickly, Jack thought. He had been too young to recognize the pattern back then. To realize that his mother always got wound up, like one of those stupid plastic toys, right before she started spinning. She could get crazy mad. So mad, so crazy, she would leave.

And now it hit him:

Mom had *left* his grandmother. Mom had left Gram.

Maybe Gram understood. Maybe she was the only other person on the planet who knew how things really were. Knew that his mom did her best but that sometimes her best wasn't enough, wasn't nearly enough.

Big Jack held out his phone to Jack.

"OK," he agreed. "But after we see Lydia."

Jack sat forward in his seat as they drove into the busy town of York, but his stomach took a dive when he saw the entrance of the park. Hardly any cars were parked out front. Definitely not a good sign.

They got out of the car and walked past silent kiddie rides, to the animal pens. "Wait here," said Big Jack, and he went into the gift shop to get their admission passes.

"No way!" said Jack. "I need to know if Lydia's here!" He followed Jack inside, where they asked the woman behind the cash register.

"Well," she said, "Victor, one of the trainers, was in here a few minutes ago to buy a soda and say good-bye. But that doesn't mean they've pulled out yet."

Jack raced through the gate ahead of Big Jack. She couldn't be gone! She couldn't! He couldn't have come all this way, gone through so much, only to have her slip through his fingers.

There were a few families with young children strolling around the tree-lined park, peering into cages. He dodged past them, not even looking to see what animals he passed. It was enough to know they weren't elephants.

Almost immediately, the paved path forked around a small pond. Left or right? Which way?

"Go left!" shouted Big Jack, a few yards behind him.

Jack took off, tearing past couples holding hands, a kid with a balloon, more animal cages, and then—

There she was.

Lydia.

Lydia the elephant. Her trunk curled up into the air.

It was really her! He'd actually made it!

And right in front of Lydia's pen, practically camping out on a park bench, was his grandmother.

Twenty-five

Love will draw an elephant through a key-hole.
— Samuel Richardson

Jack turned to Big Jack, his eyes wild. What kind of trap was this? Had he known all along? Who would have told him about the elephant? Sylvie?

"What's wrong?" Big Jack looked past Jack and must have spotted his grandmother. "Wait a minute, kid," he said. "You don't think I—? I didn't have anything to do—"

Jack tried to push past Big Jack and run away before Gram spotted him.

But Big Jack reached for him. "Hold on, kid." He placed his hands on Jack's shoulders and gently steered him toward a different bench, one that was out of sight of his grandmother. "Sit down here for a moment. Talk to me," said Big Jack.

Jack slumped onto the wooden bench and refused to meet Big Jack's eyes.

"Listen," said Big Jack. "I was a foster kid. Bounced from house to house. My mother would be able to take us back for a while, and then something would go wrong and we'd be living with a family we'd never met. So I know a little about what you're feeling. About the powerlessness, and the shame."

"It was *my* fault she left. The fight—"

But Big Jack was already shaking his head. "No way, kid. It took me a long time to realize that things weren't my fault. That I wasn't the one in control. That no matter what I did, the consequences would probably have been the same. And it's hard, I know; you don't want to give yourself over to the people who are willing to take you in—*take care of you*—because it feels like you're betraying your own mother."

Jack stared at his lap. "I am." His voice was barely a whisper.

"You heard about the man who called your grandmother from the boat, right?"

Jack nodded.

"Who do you think gave that guy your grandmother's phone number?"

Jack looked up. "Mom?"

"That's right. She may have been manic, but she was taking care of you, kid."

Jack and Big Jack sat silently for a few moments. Jack pulled out his elephant and held it in his hands. He remembered lying on the elephant rock on Mount Desert Island—how sturdy it had felt beneath him, how comforting it had felt to have the warm sun on his back. He looked up at Big Jack.

"You ready?" Big Jack asked.

Jack took a few deep breaths. Finally, he nodded, got up, and walked over to his grandmother.

Would she be angry at him for running away, for not calling her and telling her what had happened? So angry that she wouldn't want him?

But the moment she looked up and saw him coming down the path, he knew he didn't have to worry. Not about that.

"Jack!" she yelled, like she couldn't believe he was there, like all she'd wanted in the world was to see him and know he was safe. She ran toward him, her arms wide, and he threw himself into her embrace.

He couldn't believe it. He was crying for the third time that day.

Elephants love reunions. They recognize one another after years and years of separation and greet each other with wild, boisterous joy. There's bellowing and trumpeting, ear flapping and rubbing. Trunks entwine.

Jack didn't need any of those things to know that Gram wasn't mad. That quite possibly she understood even more than he did.

The two of them sat down on her bench together. Jack could tell that his grandmother wanted to ask loads of questions but wasn't sure where to begin.

"Who told you I'd be here?" asked Jack.

"No one," said Gram. "Every day I've gotten calls telling me you've been seen—I got one from the Waldoboro Police Department today—but no one, no one, has been able to find you."

"Then what are you doing here?" he asked. It seemed like too big a coincidence.

"It was my only hope," said Gram. "The only place in Maine I thought you might choose to come to. I've been right here with Lydia all week."

Jack looked up to where Lydia was, hidden just around a bend. He still couldn't believe he was actually here, that he'd actually made it. "I knew I had to see her," he said. "As soon as I realized I couldn't make it back to JP, I knew this was where I had to go. I thought if Mom found out, it might remind her of the time she took me to see an elephant. And that she might understand that I was OK. That I still loved her." He wondered if any of that had made sense.

Gram's eyes got teary, and he knew she understood. "You know, *I* took you to see an elephant once, too," she said. "Of course, you wouldn't remember," she added. "You were such a little thing when I took you to the circus. You hated being in the big top, hated the clowns, but oh, how you loved the elephant!"

Blood *whoosh*ed in his ears. It was *Gram* who had taken him? Not Mom?

"It was like you were long-lost playmates," she continued. "'*Phant* was one of your first words."

Jack was still trying to adjust his memories. Maybe that was why his mom had eventually stopped sharing his love of elephants — because she was so angry at Gram. If it weren't for Gram, he wouldn't have been obsessed with elephants in the first place.

Another memory struck him. "Do you still have the elephant bed?" asked Jack.

"You remember *that*?" Gram looked astounded.

"The posts reminded me of an elephant's legs."

"You always looked so small in that great big bed."

Jack looked at the ground and rocked from side to side. "Will that . . . will that bed be—?" He couldn't bring himself to ask the question.

Gram seemed to read his mind. "Will that bed be yours now? Is that what you were going to ask?"

Jack nodded.

"If it fits," said Gram.

Jack looked up at her, not sure what she meant.

"I was actually thinking I might sell the big

house in Cambridge, move to a smaller one in Jamaica Plain. You could stay with me and still attend the same school—with Nina! Goodness, Nina—she's worried sick about you, you know."

Nina. He was surprised to find that thinking about her no longer made him angry. He could see now that she'd done what she thought was best— what probably *was* best. And a part of him was actually looking forward to seeing her again. He could hear her voice, egging him on to tell her about all of his crazy adventures: *Once upon a time . . .*

"And as your mom gets better," said Gram. "Well, then, you'd have two homes to go to."

Jack felt light-headed with hope. "Mom will be allowed to come home?"

"Well, she will probably have to stay in the hospital for a time—"

"Not jail?" breathed Jack.

"Oh, no! You mother wasn't in her right mind, Jack. She needs a place where they can help her get better. Get better and *stay* better. Stay better for you."

Jack fought back tears. He wouldn't cry again,

not about something happy. Instead, he hugged his grandmother, gripping her as tight as he dared. When he finally let go, he saw Big Jack approaching. He ran to greet him. Gram followed.

"This is *Big* Jack. He brought me here."

"Another Jack!" Gram said, taking hold of Big Jack's arm. "I can't thank you enough."

"It was my pleasure," said Big Jack. He turned to Jack. "I just called the police to let them know that you've been found, that you're with your grandmother. All of the news stations will be rushing to get the story. *Your life* is going to be a zoo for a few days."

Jack nodded. "Would you do me a favor?" he asked.

"Another one, kid? You're really pushing your luck here." But he was smiling.

Jack laughed. He pulled the elephant from his pocket. He studied it for a moment, running his fingers over its legs, its back, its ears, and, finally, its raised truck. He handed it to Big Jack. "Can you give this to a girl in Searsport? Oh, and this, too," he said, remembering the ten-dollar bill that Wyatt had given him.

Big Jack nodded, and Jack gave him Sylvie's name. "I don't know her address, but if anyone can find her, it's you. Except," he added, "you can't tell anyone that I sent you, or ask her anything."

"OK," said Big Jack, clearly confused but at least willing to go along with it. "Anything you want me to say to her?"

"Tell her . . ." Jack thought for a moment. "Tell her I got it. I got my Monopoly."

Big Jack looked bemused. "Whatever you say, kid."

"And, Jack?"

"Yeah, kid?"

"Tell her the elephant's name is Mudo."

Big Jack laughed. "You got it."

And then Jack couldn't help himself. He grabbed Big Jack around the middle once more and squeezed tight.

Big Jack hugged back, and when he finally let go, he said, "Someday you're gonna be there for someone else, kid. Wait and see."

Jack just nodded, afraid that the waterworks were going to start again.

"We'll stay in touch," said Gram.

"Don't forget to say hi to Lydia," Big Jack called as he walked away. "She's waiting for you."

Lydia! Jack almost forgot!

He followed Gram back to the elephant pen. It was a small wire enclosure with a wooden hut in the middle for shelter and a platform off to the left where people could climb up some steps and then slide onto the seat on Lydia's back. Lydia was standing with her back to them. She turned as they approached, as if she'd been expecting them, and meandered closer.

Jack's heart jumped to his throat. "She looks like she's smiling, just like she did in her pictures," he said.

"She looks a bit impish, doesn't she?" asked Gram. The way she said it, Jack knew she admired impish.

Lydia walked up to the fence and picked up a large plastic container of water. She emptied it, and then she began rolling the container around on the ground.

"I think she's performing for you," said Gram.

The word *perform* made Jack think of his mother — of how she hated it when animals were made to perform. Lydia *seemed* like she was having fun as she rolled the container closer to Jack. But there she was, in that cramped little space with wire all around.

"It's too bad she's all alone," said Jack.

"She has two trainers who take care of her," said Gram. "I met them while I was waiting for you. Victor and Belinda."

"But they're not other elephants," said Jack.

"No, they're not," said Gram. "They're certainly not."

Lydia rolled the plastic bucket closer to Jack and Gram. Jack stretched out his hand, desperate to touch her.

"Would you like to ride her?"

Jack turned. A woman had walked up next to them. She wore a brown uniform. Belinda, he guessed.

Jack thought for a moment. Thought about sitting on top of this awesome creature. How he would feel so small and so tall at the same time. It would be cool to feel her back; to hug her, or try to hug her, around her neck.

Then he thought about his mother. She would never approve of his riding Lydia. And he realized something just then. He wasn't just Jack, the boy who had traveled all this way to be with an elephant. He was, and would always be, his mother's son.

"No, thanks," he said.

"You sure?" asked Gram.

Jack nodded. He was sure.

Gram smiled at him. She reached out and ruffled his hair.

Lydia walked closer, close enough for him to reach over the wire and touch her. Running his hand down her bumpy trunk gave him a shiver. He remembered what he'd heard about blowing into an elephant's trunk — how the elephant would never forget you.

What about his mother? Would she —?

Nah. Somewhere in his heart, he knew — knew that for her, forgetting would be impossible. His mother might not be able to care for him always, but she would never forget him.

Jack craned his neck to look into Lydia's eye.

"You've traveled a long way to see her," Belinda said. "Stand up on the platform there, and I'll bring her over to you. You don't have to get on. Just get a closer look."

Jack's heart pounded as he climbed the steps. Slowly, led by Belinda, Lydia met him on the other side. Jack was high enough that he could bend over to pat her on the top of her head, but instead, he lay down on his belly, so that the two of them were face-to-face. He looked into one of her huge, dark eyes, fringed by a bouquet of soft wrinkles. He reached out and was about to pat her when she raised her trunk and ran it ever so gently along his forehead and down to his ear, like a trail of gentle kisses.

Jack giggled but tried not to move. Lydia's touch was magical.

Playfully, she tapped him on the back. Her face was so close that Jack momentarily rested his cheek against her skin.

Time stood still.

I made it, Mom, he thought. *I made it all the way to Lydia. For both of us.*

Jack thought about all the people who had helped him get to this point: Aiden and his family, Big Jack, Sylvie, Wyatt. Even Mrs. Olson, who had given him vegetables, and the man at the food pantry, and the librarian in Bar Harbor, who had let him use the Internet — they'd helped him without knowing they were helping. And then there was his grandmother, camping out in an animal park, just waiting for Jack to come find her. And Nina, who had been brave enough to tell his grandmother that he needed help.

All along the way, Jack realized, he had never *really* been alone. He had been a part of a makeshift herd, one that had spread out over miles. They had communicated with heart sounds that were sometimes so soft, they weren't always discernible to the ear. But they had found one another, and they had helped one another. Just like a true herd.

"Jack, sweetie," his grandmother called, and he knew it was time to go. It didn't feel like an end-ing; nor did it feel like a beginning. It felt like the middle of a journey, one that had started long ago. It was time for the next leg.

Lydia seemed to sense it, too. She ran her trunk along his face one last time.

Jack smiled, cupped his hands gently around the tip of her trunk, and let out a gentle puff of air.

Acknowledgments

I want to express my sincerest gratitude for those who supported my journey as I wrote about Jack's. I received invaluable feedback from my trusted readers: Holly Jacobson, Jacqueline Davies, Dana Walrath, Mary Atkinson, Jane Kurtz, Nancy Werlin, Joanne Stanbridge, Jacqueline Briggs Martin, Franny Billingsley, Toni Buzzeo, and the insightful Barry Goldblatt, who also happens to be my agent. I received technical information from Erik Jacobson, John Jacobson, Mae Corrion from Jesup Memorial Library, and Lindsay McGuire of Left Bank Books. Thank you all!

Special thanks, too, to the folks that housed me (and answered all my questions) as I re-created Jack's journey along the coast of Maine: Liz Laverack and John, Sam, and Peter Jacobson, and Nancy and Don Buckingham.

Finally, I want to thank the extraordinary people at Candlewick Press: Liz Bicknell, Katharine Gehron, Maggie Deslaurier, Emily Crehan, Hannah Mahoney, Teri Keough, Kate Cunningham (who designed the gorgeous cover), Sharon Hancock, and Susan Batcheller, but most important, with unabashed adoration, my editor, Kaylan Adair, whose incredible knowledge of story and mindful attention to detail helped guide every word on these pages. Kaylan simultaneously supports and challenges her authors—a talent every writer admires, and one for which this writer will forever be grateful.

Lowell School
1640 Kalmia Road, NW
Washington, DC 20012